MW01140135

THE CLOSER

LESLIE PIKE

Copyright 2021 Leslie Pike

All Rights Reserved

Without limiting the rights under copyright reserved above, no part of this publication, may be reproduced, stored in or introduced into a retrieval system, or transmitted, in any form, or by any means (electronic, mechanical, photocopying, recording, or otherwise) without the prior written permission of both the copyright owner and the above publisher of this book.

This is a work of fiction. Names, characters, places, brands, media and incidents are either the product of the author's imagination or are used fictitiously. The author acknowledges the trademarked status and trademark owners of various products, brands, bands, and/or restaurants referenced in this work of fiction, which have been used without permission. The publication/use of these trademarks is not authorized, associated with, or sponsored by the trademark owners.

Editor: Nicole, Insight Editing
Proofreading: Leticia Sidon, In-Depth Edits
Kari March, Kari March Designs

For those who still, and always will believe in great loves

CHAPTER 1

JANUARY

*S*ilence is better than bullshit. My shrewd father used to say that whenever I'd try to weasel out of something. Years later, I found it applied to other situations. Like tonight. I'm mostly keeping my mouth shut until I get called to the stage. Zip. A few well-placed nods and an occasional laugh is all that's required when the people you're sitting with only want to talk about work. *Ad nauseam.*

It's a yawn exhibit. There's no athletes to lighten the night's mood, or coaches to share funny stories from the past. Tonight there's only people like me, agents, managers, financial planners, from both coasts and everywhere in between. In other words, the queen and kingmakers congratulating ourselves on a stellar year.

Some feed on accolades. I don't. The end result is all that's needed to validate a job well done. But I'll accept my award for the year's record-breaking contract graciously. Then I'll sneak out as soon as I don't look like an ingrate.

We may not be the most interesting group, but everyone here has the one thing our clients don't. Anonymity. The public doesn't give a damn who we are. I never realized how valuable privacy was until I witnessed people losing theirs. When you're a star athlete, you live in a gilded prison. But as the agent, I can misbehave all I want. Even right here. Not that I would.

Wish I was home putting Saturday night to good use. There's a Snickers bar in the freezer and a favorite vibrator or three in the drawer next to my bed. A girl needs variety, after all.

Instead, I'm sitting with colleagues listening to their takes on the Baseball Commissioner's divorce. Who gives a shit? I might be the first person to literally die of boredom. The headline would read, *Sports Agent Mysteriously Drops Dead.* The article would go on to say it was two hours before anyone noticed my head in the soup. They were all talking too much to hear the impact skull to bowl.

Guess I'll have to entertain myself. Cue the Jeopardy theme music and Alex Trebek's voice in my mind. *La la la la, la la la. This is January Jeopardy!* Time to play my favorite game. *Tonight's category, Fuck Buddies.* How many of the men sitting close by would I screw if given a million dollars per man? Then I'll add it up and see if I beat my last best score. *What is eight, Alex?*

The fact I came up with this pastime at seventeen only makes the diversion more interesting. My standards have changed over the last twenty-three years. Even the declining value of a million dollars alters the game.

Let's begin. This man, to my right, is normally too old for my tastes, and he may not have the ability required. But in my fantasy world, they all can get it up. Nineteen or ninety, they have a wild python in their pants. It gives the contestants an even playing field. I'd do this one. The clef in his chin is sexy. He's stayed modern. Not young, which is an impossibility, but up to date in his shoes and glasses and haircut. He has no idea I'm giving him the once over.

Now the one next to him is a definite no. Oh God, no, nyet, not gonna happen. I'd rather diddle myself with a rotten cucumber than do him. Keep the million and pay for some table manners, honey. When he eats, his tongue pushes forward, and everybody around him can see what he's chewing. Close your damn mouth, man! He thinks I'm looking at him, which I am. But most definitely not in the way he thinks. Let's move on.

The guy on the left just got up and excused himself from the table. Very slowly, I turn my head and watch him walk away. Cha-Ching! The January Jordan Fuck Fest Fund just went up. All he has to do is keep quiet. Because judging by what I heard from him tonight, he's vain. Too bad. He's got a great ass. Maybe he should be in the E.F. category. Emergency Fuckable.

Next to Mr. I'm Wonderful sits a contestant I'll have to disqualify. Mindy Myers and I have talked many times, usually over a legal issue within a contract. She's smart. But even if I liked women sexually, Mindy wouldn't be my type. I've never seen a person with such a high profile job look so disheveled. Her polish is worn, and lipstick has smeared just a little into the lines above her lips. When she wiped her mouth on the napkin a minute ago, it only made things worse. It looks like she colored outside the lines.

Sometimes when playing, I let the women participate. If the pickings are especially thin, I factor the ladies in and imagine what I'd do to them for a million dollars. It seems like an awful lot of detail work for the money.

And what if the tables were turned and I was the one being judged? That's a horrible thought. I've got too many flaws to count. My ears are too big, breasts too small. My second toe is longer than the big one. No to mention...wait. What the hell? This is my fantasy game, not theirs. I chuckle a little.

The man on my right glances over. Instead of returning the stare, I casually look to the left through the empty seat, towards the other tables.

That's when I see him studying me with a crooked smile. Oh

shit. How long has that been going on? Was I making peculiar expressions as I appraised possible conquests? A smirk? Maybe a random shake of the head or a lifted eyebrow? He probably thinks I have Tourette's.

Hands-on his lap, he runs his right index finger slowly over his lifted left. Three times. There's a flush creeping up my face, and I'm pressing my lips together, but I hold his stare. That's Brick Swift, scolding me like he read my dirty girl thoughts. He's one of the most respected sports agents here. I know his roster includes his brother Atticus and a handful of other top tier athletes.

I've been meaning to call and introduce myself since I arrived in Memphis. Now my hope for a professional first impression is missed. But it appears he's got a sense of humor to go along with that hot body wearing the expensive suit.

My eyebrows raise, sending him an acknowledgment. I get a nod and a smile and return the same. He looks away. What a face. Nice smile. Sexy. If I was in the market, I'd buy twelve cases of whatever that man's selling, and sign up for automatic refills. I'm not shopping, though. But just for the purpose of the game, it's a hell yes I'd do Brick Swift. And the million dollars? Can I bank two if I do him twice and throw in a blowjob?

~

"Thank you," I say, holding up my engraved Waterford bowl and giving a quick wave to the crowd. The two-minute acceptance speech seemed like it took an hour. Blah, blah, blah, thank you.

Their applause dies down as I make my way off the stage. By the time the host wraps up the presentation, and the voices of resumed conversations rise, I see who's sitting at my table. In the previously empty chair next to mine is the two million dollar man. As I approach, he stands.

"Hello, January. I'm Brick," he says with a warm smile and an outstretched hand.

"Your good reputation precedes you. It's really nice to finally meet," I say, shaking his hand.

He holds out my chair like a southern gentleman should. Too many New York men would let me take my seat unassisted, not wanting to treat me any differently when we're on the same playing field. They think I'd object to being shown the niceties because I'm a tough broad in the boardroom. Not this man. He's one of the few who's figured out the two issues aren't mutually exclusive.

"Thank you," I say.

He signals to the wait staff nearby. When he turns back, I get a dazzling smile. "Would you like a cocktail? I'm going to have a vodka martini."

"Great idea. Make it two."

As soon as our order's in, he leans in towards me and speaks over the noise in the room. "I've been meaning to call and introduce myself."

"You stole my opening line. It's me who should have called you. It's just that things have been so hectic these first months back in Memphis."

"Back?" He looks surprised. "I thought you were a native New Yorker."

"I've lived and worked there for seventeen years. Ever since I graduated from law school. But I'm a Tennessee girl born and raised. I'm here for three more months to put my parents' house up for sale.

"So, you're bi-coastal now."

"New York will always be home base. But I'll fly here as needed."

"Congratulations, by the way on the Jon McMartin contract. He's going to be quite an addition to the Mavericks. I know my client Duane Ricky, and he are good friends."

He comes across as genuine. I don't detect a hint of envy.

"Thanks. It was a ball buster of a negotiation. If I had 'em, they'd be shriveled up to tiny prunes."

Thankfully he laughs.

"It's good that we're only a week into the postseason, so you can take a few breaths."

"I'm taking the time required to get my parents' business wrapped up. That's about all I'll have before I renegotiate for another client."

"Word is your methods bring the other big dogs to their knees," he says.

"That's just talk. I use the same weapons all agents have in their arsenals."

"I don't think so," he says matter of factly. "Or maybe you just know how to use them more effectively."

There was nothing salacious about the comment. He was acknowledging my tactics.

Our drinks are delivered, and Brick raises his to me. He sure does have lovely dark blue eyes.

"Here's to January Jordan, the new girl in town, who's entertaining to watch from afar."

He *was* watching me scope the table.

"And to Brick Swift, her new drinking friend, who seems to be good at reading women's minds."

THE NIGHT ENDED on a good note. Driving home, I'm reliving the highlights. Brick was a gentleman and walked me to my car. When I mentioned we should have lunch sometime soon, he looked pleased. I think he's one of the good guys. There's something in his eyes I can't read, though. Maybe melancholy. But from what I can see and what I've heard, he lives a charmed life.

I know the entire Swift family falls under the category of

Memphis baseball elite. People speak highly of them. I'd do well to connect with them. To that point, my focus is on doing the best I can for my clients. And part of that is building business relationships that benefit all parties. The Swifts are perfect examples. Once in a while, you make an actual friend too. Could happen for Brick and me.

All roads lead me back to this house and this Tennessee land. The street winding in through the Red Maple trees is so beautiful. I've driven it a thousand times, but still, it holds magic. In October, the foliage is especially beautiful with the vibrant colors of changing leaves.

And when the house comes into view, I get this feeling I can't replicate anywhere else. Probably it's because I know every inch of the place, land, and two-story childhood home. Love lived here. The four of us were such a happy family. How will I have the heart to sell this place? And even more disturbing is how will it feel when I'm not able to come back and walk through the rooms?

I pull in front and park the car. Walking toward the front door, I'm serenaded by the sound of crickets. It's such a comfort. Each time I return to Memphis, I notice all the small things I do without in New York. *What's that?* My eyes lock on the colorful card lying on the top step leading to the porch. When I pick it up, I'm struck by the beauty of the design, and its pristine condition. I'm pretty sure this is a tarot card. How did it wind up here? A naked dancing woman is the central figure, and she's surrounded by a green wreath of flowers. The words The World announces its' name. I tuck the card inside my coat pocket. Maybe I'll Google it later. My sister, the Sultana of Signs from beyond, will want to see it too.

Entering the house and turning on the lights, I'm hit with the reality of what's missing. My parents are both gone now. Our precious Sammy, the family dog that lived to old age, long passed too. Their absence has left a hole in my heart, but not within these walls. I still feel its spirit comfort and wrap around me, saying *You're home.*

That's the biggest reason I'm hesitating selling. I've never had the same feeling in any other house or condo or apartment. No matter how much I loved them, they didn't feel like home. I could buy my sister out, that's always an option. I know she'd love it because she's as attached to our ghosts as I am. They're all still here on some level. So great was their connection to this place on Earth and to my sister and me.

Now with my father recently gone, there's a whole lot of clearing out we need to do. Three big boxes in the entry are the only evidence I've even started the job I volunteered for. I couldn't let my very pregnant sister bear the load alone.

"Oh god," I sigh to the empty room.

Heading for the kitchen, I toss my purse to the wooden counter. The cell sounds. Someone's texting. I grab a water from the refrigerator and the Snickers from the freezer. Retrieving my purse, I head upstairs.

Halfway up, the phone reminds me there's a message, so I dig for the cell and look. A smile breaks out on my face. It's Brick.

How about lunch today? Let's get to know each other.

I check my watch. It's one minute past midnight. I sit myself down on the staircase.

"Were you waiting for the clock to turn before typing 'today'?

There's a pause before he responds.

"Yes. How is it that you've figured me out already?"

I laugh out loud.

"Sure, lunch sounds good. I'm free around two. Does that work?"

He's typing.

"Two it is. Italian or Sushi?"

"Definitely Italian."

"Shall we meet at Giovanni's on Third?"

"It's one of my favorites."

"See you there."

And that's it. For a minute, I thought he was going to make a play. There's no part of me that's interested in mixing business and pleasure. But I have a good feeling about the man. We could be friends. He's smart and speaks softly, and he has that certain unforced something that connects with my personality. Besides the fact I can tell he thinks I'm funny. I like that.

CHAPTER 2

BRICK

The satisfying aroma of coffee surrounds me as soon as I walk into Starbucks. I spot Atticus at the small corner table. It must have been his only choice because he looks like he's too big for the space. His baseball cap is over his eyes in an attempt to stay incognito.

It's crowded today. At least five people are on their laptops and more on their cells. The only person without a technology crutch is my friend, the old guy whose name I don't know. He sits waiting patiently for me to send over his daily coffee and pastry. He's always alone and never makes eye contact. Not till he walks out. That's when I get a nod. From the beginning, he let me know he didn't want to talk. He's always neat and clean, although his clothes are timeworn. But I'm not sure there's anyone in his life to notice.

"Make it the usual for my friend, and I'll have a Grande. Black," I say to the upbeat kid who sees me more regularly than anybody in my life. "And a bran muffin."

"Sure thing, Mr. Swift."

Atticus lifts his chin in his usual hello. I answer the same way. The shorthand of our conversations would make a good body language study. I'm handed my order and make my way through the tables.

"Hey, brother," he says as I take a seat.

"How's your morning going?"

"I'm fortifying myself for today's wedding projects. Actually, it's the reception. The wedding we agreed on right away."

I chuckle at his expression. It's the one most of the men I've known wear when it comes to planning parties of any kind. Resignation. I don't think it's in our DNA.

"What's on today's list?"

"Flowers." He rolls his eyes with the thought and lets out a big sigh.

"Sounds exciting," I say dryly.

"If I didn't love Charlotte so much, I'd say let's have a barbecue and wear our flip flops. I just want to be married. But she has her heart set on a proper party, as she calls it. And Mallory's all in. They never run out of things to get excited about. The invitations, the seating chart, the three thousand Bride magazines around the house."

"Your own family would disown you if didn't celebrate. Nine more weeks, right?"

"Yeah. You haven't asked me what hot women will be there. Don't you want to know?" he says.

"No. Doesn't matter. Whatever."

He looks me in the eye. "You act like you're a hundred years old, Brick. You gonna bring someone?"

"I'll think about it when it gets closer."

He can read my face. It's telling him to change the subject.

"Okay. We have to talk about the bachelor party. I don't want one."

"Really?"

"What's the point? I've had my fill of that kind of shit."

My eyes widen. "That's the first time you've ever said those words."

He chuckles and shrugs. "It's the Charlotte effect. Now tell me what you're up to today. Negotiating a contract or putting out a fire somewhere?"

"Not really. I'm meeting an agent for lunch."

He stops talking for a beat, then narrows his eyes. "Who's that? Why the look on your face?"

It surprises me. "What look? It's our new second baseman's agent, January Jordan. But it's a business lunch."

Lifting his nose in the air, he sniffs for an imaginary scent. "I knew it was about a woman. I can smell it a mile away, "

"It's not about a woman, asshole. Quit reading into things."

"Nice way to talk to your little brother. What's she look like? Your type?"

"Like a woman. I didn't really pay too much attention."

I almost start laughing before he does because when Atticus thinks he's picked up a scent, he keeps digging. It's easier to answer him the first time.

"Really, it's just good business," I continue. "She's representing McMartin, and who's his good friend that I know?"

"I have no idea."

"Duane Rick, the Atlanta Braves' favorite trouble maker. My client."

He's weighing the facts and deciding whether to believe me or not. I'm getting the once over as if he can decipher the truth just by looking.

"Okay. I guess it makes sense," he says, temporarily giving up.

"Yeah, it does. We need to make sure those two don't get into trouble."

"Good luck with that. Answer my question. What does she look like?"

"Blonde. Tall. About 5'10". Blue eyes, kinda like a lake. Nice body. She's got this voice..."

"But you didn't really pay attention, huh?"

"Shut up," I say, holding back a smile.

All Atticus does is grin and nod, like he just rutted out the truffle.

* * *

GLAD JANUARY PICKED ITALIAN. Now if she'd only show up so we can get to it. I check the time. Twenty minutes past two.

"Can I get you another glass of wine, Mr. Swift?

"No, Anthony. I'll wait till my party joins me."

That's when I see her walking through the door. I and every other guy in the restaurant. Their eyes are locked on the woman in white. Great tailored suit. Fits her to a T. I take it all in before she has a chance to bust me looking. It's funny watching the drooling men, and the way she walks past them. It's a kind of saunter. But not at all put on. I think her body just was made to move well.

As soon as she passes the eyes of more than a few of the men slowly lower to ass gazing height. Men are such idiots. We think we're being sly. I'd guess she knows they're looking. She's probably used to being ogled. There's nothing sexier than a woman who has it all to display but instead keeps it undercover. Imagination's a turn-on.

I watch her speaking to Anthony. Looks like they know each other. He stands a little straighter in her presence, but it might be because he's at least six inches shorter.

Fact is she's striking. The whole package works well together. I'm going to keep that to myself. If Atticus or anyone in my family heard me say that I'd never hear the end of it. People close to me are hungry to see me with someone, and they don't hide it. Giving them false hope just because I admire what a woman looks like would be a mistake.

Her eyes find mine. A grin lifts the corners of her mouth.

"Hi! Sorry, I'm late. It's not like me," she says approaching.

I stand, and we exchange cheek kisses. Nice subtle perfume.

The heels she's wearing lift her to my height, six one. I hold out her chair.

"That's good to hear because being late is my pet peeve," I say.

She gets comfortable in her seat and looks over her shoulder back at me.

"You'd better buckle up then buttercup. I lied. Being late is occasionally like me. But only when I'm meeting friends. Never when it's concerning business."

I sit. "Well, the good news is I'm in the friend category."

"You are. God help you," she chuckles.

"Are you hungry? Or are you a lettuce and water type?"

"I'm not sure you're going be able to categorize me that easily, Brick."

Anthony walks up, and she speaks before he has a chance to ask what she'd like.

"I'm starving, Anthony. I'll start with the Caesar salad. For the entrée, I think the Fettuccini sounds good. And will you bring out some of your bread with olive oil and vinegar," she pauses. "Oh! Are you having a cocktail?" She asks me.

"Of course. I'm off for the rest of the afternoon."

She touches my hand in solidarity.

"Me too! We can get hammered." She says it so sweetly as if she's suggesting we partake in a Shirley Temple binge. I'm not sure if she's kidding or not.

Anthony finds her charming and laughs out loud. "Let me bring you both something special. My bartender's drink for lovers."

"You can bring it, but you better make it the friend version, "she says. "You know. Just a drop more of alcohol."

"I'll have what she's having," I say, wondering if she gets the reference.

When Anthony walks away, she turns and dips her chin. Her beautiful blues look up at me. "Please tell me you're quoting "When Harry Met Sally.""

"I am."

"It's my favorite movie from puberty. I thought it was the sexiest thing ever made. Even though I was too young to know what I was talking about."

I nod. "My mother had the VHS tape. When I was about ten, I'd watch the scene where Sally fakes an orgasm over and over. Stop. Rewind. Play.

"What a little pervert. Did you learn anything?" She giggles.

"Not really. I was under a crushing handicap. First, I needed to figure out what an orgasm was."

And that was how our afternoon started. With talk of faked orgasms and getting hammered. We discussed movies and music and our shared love of good food and cheap candy. We hardly touched on the most obvious mutual interest, our jobs.

Hours passed quickly, and it wasn't just the alcohol and Italian feast that made the conversation so damned easy. It was her company. I've never seen someone enjoy a meal so much. You'd have thought we were in Italy dining at the best Michelin rated restaurant. It made the experience fun.

I knew we were going to get along. But I didn't know I'd end up liking her so much in the course of an afternoon. I'm totally at ease with the woman. Making friends slowly has been my m.o., at least since Katy died. It takes me a while to warm up to people. I'm sure it's because I've got such a cold place inside my heart. Today there's been a small thaw.

"I'm stuffed!" she says, leaning her head back. "Just enough room left for dessert."

"You have the appetite of an elephant."

"How rude!" she laughs. "You're a little tipsy, aren't you?"

"Damned it, that may be true," I say, swallowing the burp that wanted to escape.

"Damned it? Did you say damned it?"

"I'm pretty sure I did." I chuckle, and she joins me. I lean in

15

closer. "Why am I the only one getting hammered? I know! It's because all that food in your stomach soaked up the alcohol."

"It couldn't possibly be the cocktails and wine you had."

"This never happens. Really."

"Let loose. Have some more lasagna. You barely touched it."

My hand comes up. "No, I'm good. Would you like mine?" Not really thinking she'd say yes.

"I might have just a forkful," she says, reaching across the table and taking another serving.

"I'm not much of a cook. That's a gross understatement. I hate it," she says.

"I enjoy it. Got that from my grandmother, Birdie. She's the best cook in a family of cooks."

"Grandma Birdie. Great name."

"She's one of a kind."

"So do you cook just for yourself? Every night?" she says, wrinkling her nose as if it would be a horrible fate.

"Not every night. Maybe three times a week. And are you asking if I'm single?" I say, grinning.

"If I was, you'd know it. I'd say. 'Are you single?'.

Okay, she's sort of awesome.

"What about you?" I ask." Just so I'm not blindsided in the parking lot by some bodybuilder in a jealous rage."

"First of all, yes, I'm single and dating. Nothing serious. Second of all, what makes you think I'd be with a bodybuilder?" She grimaces with the thought.

"You look like the kind of woman that would enjoy being bench pressed."

There's a beat and then her infectious laughter.

"That's hysterical …bench pressed," she says, the corners of her mouth staying up.

I can't help but chuckle. The alcohol has loosened me up. Don't know where that comment came from, but it was a pretty good one. Very unlike me.

"Let me cook for you. Something Southern and rich. What about one night next week?" The words just poured out of my mouth, without planning or forethought.

"Yes. Okay. Know what Brick?" she says, sizing me up," I think we're about to become friends. I kinda like you."

Her gaze is straightforward.

"That's what I was thinking too. Did we just hit it off?" I grin.

"Like Harry and Sally. Except we'll prove a man and a woman *are* capable of being just friends."

"Agreed. Let's ignore the fact it didn't work for them," I say.

One eyebrow lifts. "That was because they let sex ruin everything."

"We're smarter than that. They were younger and dumber than we are. "

"How old are you?" she asks.

"I turn forty-one next month. How about you? Or is that an indelicate question?"

"What? Why would it be?"

Her eyes are sending me death rays.

"I don't know! It's something men usually don't ask outright."

"I'm forty fucking years old."

"Forty fucking years look good on you," I grin.

"Thank you. I'm in the prime of my life." She pauses." I say that no matter how old I am."

"Good plan. I wished I believed it for myself."

"There's a lot in life to be dazzled by. Don't you think?"

"My dazzle meter needs recalibrating."

"Enjoying life is what makes me feel young. So I leave room for play and pleasure."

She notices the dirty direction my mind and expression just took.

"Not just that kind. I like playing games and swimming in the pond on our property, or walking the hills. I love eating things that taste of butter and chocolate. It's important not to miss the things that make life worthwhile."

"It's a noble goal, but hard to achieve in our profession. Work seems to take all the time I've got."

She touches my hand for just a few seconds. "Then you're working too hard. Or maybe you just can't remember how great it feels to step away for a few hours and not have to be "the guy.""

"Maybe."

"I don't know about you, but I get tired of being the person with the answers."

Her hands lift in the air like a convert testifying in a church. "I've got it! Let's have game night at my place."

"I'm not a game player. No," I state emphatically.

"Come on! If we're gonna be biddies, we should learn about what each likes. Besides, we've got to repair your dazzle meter."

"I bet you'd be good at that."

She doesn't shy away from my not so hidden meaning.

"I may have the right tools," she teases seductively.

For a long few beats, we just stare at each other with shit-eating grins. Then she breaks the spell and returns us to reality.

"You can do your cooking thing, and we can play some games. And cocktails. There's gotta be cocktails."

"You're a faux drinker," I say.

"What the hell's that?"

"You talk a big game, but we've been here what, four hours and you've nursed two drinks. And that's after promising me we'd get hammered."

Her eyes widen, and she takes a long look. An index finger points in my direction and wiggles. "But it's the possibility of it happening that's the most fun, right?"

CHAPTER 3

JANUARY

"*O*hhhhhhh!" Our voices rise in sync with the changing image projected on the screen. Sitting close together on my couch, my sister and I are holding hands, helping each other bear the impact of memories. If it wasn't for the pregnant stomach, I'd say she almost looks sixteen. A honey-colored ponytail and young face contradict her thirty-eight years.

Looking back at us from 1981 are our parents and grandparents Nana and Papa. I'm standing in front of them in my yellow Easter dress, stylin' my Lady Diana haircut. In my hands is Blue Bunny, the favorite toy given to me that year by Nana. His pristine fur and bright color didn't last long because he was loved too well to stay new. Summer's asleep in our Papa's arms.

A sibling is the only person in your life who shares your childhood years from the same vantage point. When you're only eighteen months apart, even more so. Both of us are sentimental. We don't want to let go of anything. Memories especially.

We're trying to hold back the tears that threaten to blur our slideshow, but what we see is too emotional. I catch a few streaming down Summer's face as I wipe mine with the back of my hand. Then we laugh a little at ourselves for self-inflicting the pain.

"We're masochists," says Summer.

To watch our mother's lovely face is overwhelming. I can almost hear the sound of her laughter. To see Dad's beloved golf outings and captured moments from walks with Sammy is precious. And all four of us together floating on rafts in the pond. That just about kicks me in the gut. The four of us were like a really small gang. One for all and all for one. God help anybody who'd try to hurt one of us.

My sister and I vowed to begin sorting through the rooms this morning. But then Summer uncovered all seventeen boxes labeled and in perfect order. Vacations, graduations, weddings, holidays. All waiting for us to take a trip back in time.

Dad knew we'd be doing it together. When Mom died, he watched how we processed and grieved together. Everything we went through was made better by doing it side by side. He told us he was so glad we had each other and loved unconditionally. It comforted him in the final months. The greatest gift our parents ever gave us was each other.

"Hold on. I want to get another water," Summer says, attempting to get up any way she can.

"Stay put! I'll get it."

She sits back with a grateful expression. Or maybe it's just resignation. Six months into her third pregnancy, she's ready to meet the twins and get back in her bikini.

"Mom and Dad look so young. They're younger than we are now. By a decade," she says, looking back.

I grab her a water and get a root beer for me.

"Shit. Is that true? Want an ice cream bar?"

"Bring me an Eskimo Pie. Hey, what's that Tarot card on the refrigerator?"

"Oh, I wanted to show you that. It was lying on the porch step when I got home the other night. I have no idea how it got there."

She holds out her hand and wiggles her fingers. "Let me see. It's a sign, you know. Maybe Mom and Dad are trying to communicate with us."

"I knew you were going to say that. Here, you take it. "

Summer swipes the card right from my hand and studies it. "I'll find out its meaning. We need to interpret it correctly."

She sticks it into her purse as I get our bars. Then she turns her attention to the stack of boxes on the coffee table, reading the stickers on each one.

"Let's watch this one!" She holds up a box. "January and Summer's dates from 1995 to 2000."

"Oh my god. Do you remember seeing those before?" I say, sitting back on the couch.

"No!"

She sets the carousel in its place, and with her ice cream in one hand and the remote in the other, she starts the show.

As soon as the first image comes on the screen, we burst out laughing.

"My god, January! Think you got your hair big enough?"

I pretend I'm going to punch her in the arm. "That was the style in 1995, asshole!"

"The dress! What were you thinking? You look like a cheap underaged hooker."

"Give me that!" I say, grabbing the remote.

When I click the button and a new slide projects on the screen, I start screaming. Summer does a spit take with her mouthful of Eskimo Pie. A piece of it lands on the coffee table.

"I'm gonna pee my pants. I swear I'm gonna pee," she says, for some reason holding her stomach.

"Who the hell are you with there, Ms. Lauper? Justin Timberlake's understudy?" I say. "Nice perm."

"Shut up. He was a sweet boy. Poor thing, he farted once while we were slow dancing."

"Stop! Stop!" I scream. "That's hysterical!"

Just when our tears are drying up the bulb in the projector flickers.

"Shit!" We say in unison.

I make like I know what I'm doing and jiggle the carousel. It fixes things.

"We'll have to get a new bulb. This one isn't gonna last."

The cell on the couch rings, so I turn off the projector and grab a napkin to wipe my tears of laughter.

"See who it is," I say.

Summer picks up the phone and eyes the screen. "Who's Brick?"

I come to her a little eager to sell disinterest. "I'll take it," I say, wiggling my fingers.

Bringing the cell to my ear, I sit next to my sister, who's listening intently.

"Hi," I say.

My sister mimes my suddenly sexy voice. She throws in the moony eyes.

"Afternoon," he says.

"Are you sober yet?"

Summer's eyes widen, and her jaw drops. I reject her assumption with a wave of my hand.

"God, I hope so. It's been a week. What I am is embarrassed."

"Don't be silly. You were great company." I giggle.

I'm aware my sister is watching me twirl the end of my hair. She's smirking and nodding like she's just uncovered something I'm trying to hide. I give her a silent message to stop with the glaring eyes. One middle finger raised high.

"Listen, I just got back from visiting my family. I have some Pecan fudge bars I think you'd like. Will you be going to your office later? I could drop them off."

"No. My sister's here for the next few days, and I'll be working from home. Why don't you come over? I'll make you a Lean Cuisine."

He laughs. God, that's a sexy sound.

"I think I can come up with something better. What about I cook for you two tonight?"

"Sounds good. Summer was going to have to settle for a sandwich, so she'll be happy."

Summer gives me a lopsided grin.

"And Brick, get your ass over here with those bars. Now that I know you have them, it's all I'm gonna think about."

"Okay. Send me your address. I'll be leaving in half an hour."

"Perfect. See you then."

"Oh! You have pots and pans, right?" he says.

"Of course, I have pots and pans. Do you think I use a hot plate and a tin cup?"

"It wasn't out of the realm of possibility," he laughs. "See you soon."

I disconnect and turn to face my sister. Her mouth falls open and eyes widen.

"We have pots and pans, right?" I say.

"You're inviting a man into the inner sanctum?"

"What're you talking about?" As if I didn't know. "He's just a friend."

"And he's cooking for us?"

"Yep."

"Help me up," she says, giving me an outstretched hand. I steady myself to lift her from the couch.

"That's good. I need to move. Now tell me about this Brick guy."

"He's an agent. One of the best. He introduced himself at the award ceremony last week. Nice guy, you'll like him. That's about it."

"Who do you think you're kidding?" She asks, taking a lap around the living room. "You're into him, I can tell, January."

"I swear, I'm not!" I chuckle. "Quit exaggerating."

"Don't you think I know your tells? Twirling your hair, biting your bottom lip. The goofy giggle. You're transparent as hell."

"The heat's frying your brain cells. Let's go down to the pond and cool off."

"What about your 'friend,'" she says, lifting her hands in air quotes.

"I'll leave him a note. And when I text him the address, I'll tell him to bring his trunks."

* * *

FLOATING on a big rubber tube in the family pond is therapy. The trees surrounding the water's edge are on display. All shades of crimson and gold leaves reflect in the water. Summer stretches out on the deck atop one of the red cushioned chaise lounges, reading People magazine.

I'm trying to meditate. Fingers trail in the dark blue water, and my eyes are closed against the afternoon sun. I'm pretending to be a tiny fairy riding atop a lily pad. It's surprisingly effective at carrying me away.

Music over the sound system helps set the mood. Right now, I'm sailing along to Blake Shelton.

When my parents were alive, the playlist was heavy on the Beatles and Stones, Donna Summer and The Bee Gees. As my sister and I grew into teenagers, we commandeered the system and filled it with our choices. Now it's a combination of all of our favorites. Because with age comes a wider vision, of music and just about everything else you think you know.

"Someone's coming down the path," Summer calls.

The sound of flip flops on the stone steps confirms her suspicion.

I open my eyes against the bright sunlight, and it takes a moment for them to adjust. When they do, I see the vision standing before us. He's one hell of a good looking guy. And he's only got his trunks on. They fall a bit low, exactly where God intended.

Solid muscles, flat stomach, and those arms. They're a work of art. It's only an observation. It's perfectly natural to notice a body so beautiful. It doesn't mean anything. *Why am I trying to convince myself?*

"Afternoon, ladies," Brick calls.

"Hi! I'm January 's sister, Summer," she says, throwing the magazine to the ground." I'd get up, but it'd be nightfall by the time I made it."

"I'm Brick. Stay where you are," he grins, holding up his hand and spreading his fingers.

Crossing to her side, they shake hands.

He turns and gives me the once over. "Hello to the lady in blue."

Walking towards the edge of the pond, he can't see what my sister's doing behind his back. She knows I can see her fanning herself and making like he's so hot she might faint. I almost burst out laughing when she pretends to be riding him like a cowboy on a bucking bronc, waving an imaginary Stetson.

I kick my feet and paddle my hands through the water, coming towards where he stands.

"Hi. Wanna join me? The cool water feels wonderful."

He kicks off his flip flops and starts in. "A Tennessee pond with a beautiful blonde. I could get used to this world."

When I look at my sister, her eyes are wide, and she's mouthing the word "World!"

CHAPTER 4

BRICK

*G*ood thing I'm waist-deep in water. The sight of January in that tiny bikini's waking up the rocket. And a distant voice is telling me life just got more complicated. *Just friends, just friends, just friends.* If I'm being real, I'd admit there's something different about her. No, that's not it. What's happening is there's something different about me whenever I'm with her.

The vision here requires no imagination at all. She's got exceptionally hot long legs. Her breasts are smallish, and they torment me with their perfect shape. What's her ass like? Maybe I'll turn over that inner tube and find out.

I talk big. Instead, I'll silently admire the view and act like a gentleman. The water's cold against my warm skin. I swim up to her and rest my arms on the edge of the tube. I don't miss the once over she gives em. Mostly unintentionally, my biceps flex.

"What a great spot."

"My father built this whole thing before we were born," she says with a wave of her hand.

"How far back does it go?"

Rolling off the tube, she disappears underwater, comes up, and pushes the tube away. The beads of water on her lips, the hair

26

slicked back, it looks striking. Taking a long side stroke, she calls back to me. "Come on, let me show you."

We swim together under the wooden bridge that spans across the water. From a pool house on a deck to a field of wildflowers on the opposite shore, the entire scene amazes. As we pass, butterflies and birds fly among the flowers. It feels like I'm in an animated film.

Rounding the jutting landmass with a huge Magnolia tree at its edge, the entire rock-lined natural pool is revealed. Impressive. And big enough to use the rowboat that's tied to the shore. Up ahead and on each side of the pond are water plants. They take up a good three feet of shore all around. On the land, in the water, growing and floating.

And dead center in the water is a sun deck big enough for two chaise lounges and an umbrella.

"I can't believe this place, January."

"The plants filter the water naturally." She smiles and heads for the platform. "Let's lay out. I'll tell you all about it."

Smoothly she moves ahead of me, and her strokes are even and long. I hold back so I can watch when she climbs onto the deck. Reaching it, her hands grab onto the handles of the side ladder. She gracefully lifts herself out of the water. By that time, I'm right behind her, taking in the awesome view. The fabric of her bikini bottom is wedged between two round cheeks. And the crack of her ass is showing just an inch or two. *How much can a man take?*

"Quit looking at my ass, Swift," she says without turning around.

The comment shocks me back to reality. "Well, then quit having such a good one."

She laughs out loud. Then she's atop the deck staring down at me.

"Come on. Get up here."

"Give a man a minute," I say, paddling in the water.

It takes her a few moments to figure out the reason for my hesitation. It's an embarrassing situation, but I can't help smiling.

"You do not! I don't believe you," she gasps.

The way she's looking at me, the setting, her body, the face, the water coursing over her hills, and down her valleys, it's only making things worse. So I lift myself out and stand in front of her, dripping water.

"Full disclosure ," I say.

Eyes dart to my trunks, and the tent pole pointed in her direction. She chuckles and runs her right index finger over her left one, scolding me three times.

"Naughty, naughty, naughty boy."

"You've only yourself to blame."

"You've got something in your hair. Want me to get it out?" Her voice drips with innocence. But the eyes, those are saying something completely different.

"Do it. Please."

She picks a piece of a flower out of my hair and sends a charge up my spine. We lock eyes. She's biting her bottom lip.

I look over my chest for something else for her to remove. *Please be there.*

"Think there's something here," I point to the blade of grass stuck to the edge of my nipple.

She pauses for a moment, then delicate fingers glide over the blade, barely making contact. It flutters off in the breeze. She smiles. My nipple hardens right along with my dick.

Taking her into my arms, I let her in on my idea. "There's no reason we can't just kiss,"

It didn't work for Billy Crystal and Meg Ryan." She protests without moving away.

"What do they know? Come on, we need to seal the contract," I say with conviction.

"Which contract is that?"

"The Friend Agreement. It states our terms and conditions. Addendum one allows for kissing."

The corners of her mouth turn up. "How many addendums are there?"

"I'll let you know."

My lips touch hers. Softly at first. Her hands lift to my face, and her wet, nearly naked body arches against mine. And then it happens. Everything a kiss should be exists in this moment. I've a sense of being in a place that feels unmistakably new.

When we part lips, her eyes lift to mine. For a few moments, neither of us speaks. I'm pretty sure she's as stunned as I am.

"It's a shame we're not soulmates," she murmurs.

I'm lost in the cool blue of her eyes. Then the world calls us back. A dinner bell's sounding, like the ones in an old Western.

"That's Summer. We have to get back."

"Don't pull away. Not yet," I plead.

"It's our signal. Let's go."

She grabs my face in her hands and kisses me once more. Then she dives off the platform, leaving me with a smile on my face and a hard-on in my trunks. I dive into the cool water and follow her lead back to reality.

By the time we go under the bridge, I see why the bell rang. There's a man standing on the deck, waiting and watching. When January spots him, she slows her strokes and waits for me to catch up.

"Who's that?"

"Richard. My high school boyfriend. We're friends now."

My expression hardens.

"Stop it," she says firmly.

Her face lowers halfway under the water, trying to hide the fact she's smiling. Godamn it. She's enjoying my reaction.

"What's so amusing?"

Lifting her grinning face slowly from the water, she answers. "What do you care who he is?"

"I don't," I say, shrugging.

"Uh-huh," she giggles.

And off she swims, towards the shore. I watch her rise from the pond. The asshole's standing there in his preppy shorts and polo shirt, wearing a ridiculous look on his stupid face. Wipe the drool off, man. He might be her friend, but this guy wants more. It's obvious as hell. I want to hear what they're saying, but I head in slowly, making sure to look like I don't care.

Standing in the shallow I hear January say, "Thank you, Richard, I'm sure they're lovely.

I look around for signs of a gift but can't see a thing. Back atop the chaise, fingers braided behind her head, Summer's getting a kick out of the two men vying for her sister's attention. She's enjoying the circus.

The guy's watching me and listening to January at the same time. His eyes dart between us. I'm giving him a stone-cold look. And I can't really explain why. I barely know the woman, and I don't know this guy at all. *What's happening?*

January turns to me. "Brick, I'd like you to meet my friend Richard. Richard, this is Brick."

Both of us heard the word friend. I'm happy. He's not.

"Nice to meet you, Dick," I say, slightly emphasizing the last word.

By the vein that just popped out on his temple, I'd say he knows exactly what I did there.

"Brick, is it? Sounds like your porn name!" he volleys.

Oh, fuck you. So, we're having a pissing contest? I can play that game. I invented that game. I laugh as if he didn't hit a nerve. All the while, January's biting her bottom lip, waiting for us to blow.

"Well, it'd be appropriate, Dick. I guess it could apply. Definitely. What do you think, January?" I say, lifting an eyebrow to her. I sincerely hope he gets the wrong idea.

Summer snorts her amusement. Dick's eyes narrow, and his

mouth is set in a hard line, and January loses her smile. Oh shit. I may have gone too far.

"Okay, that's enough. Both of you, stop it," she says.

"No problem. I'm going anyway," Dick says. "I'll call you tonight, January. We can talk in private."

He gives her a peck on the cheek. Yeah, I'm watching.

"Okay, Richard. I'll be here," she says.

He turns and walks away towards the house, disappearing into the trees. I notice he didn't say goodbye to Summer. She waves energetically to the departing figure.

"Okay, bye now! It was nice seeing you too, Dick. Good talk," she says sarcastically.

I laugh, and January breaks a smile, but it may be because of her sister's comment. She turns to me.

"What the hell was that?" She says calmly.

"I just didn't care for the guy. He's too tame for you," I shrug.

There's a hint of a grin showing on her face.

"You don't have to like him. And I'd appreciate it if you leave my choice of men to me. That's the second addendum of the Friend Agreement."

"Done," I say.

But it isn't.

* * *

THREE HOURS, two showers, and a very entertaining dinner later, we're nearly finished cleaning up. I move the vase of generic red roses to the side to wipe the table. Dick's gift sucks. Doesn't he realize January is a woman who deserves something unique? Something other than the generic bouquet a kid buys his mother for her birthday at the grocery store? If I brought her flowers, they'd be exotics. Or something that lets her know I've been paying attention to who she is.

We're doing the leg work while Summer sits overseeing the

operation. It's been a nonstop conversation between the Jordan sisters and me. Summer's funny. In fact, they both are. There's a sort of shorthand to their communication, words, gestures, anticipating what the other's about to say. Just like my brother and sister and I do.

"What a meal! The best I've had in years," January says, popping the last bite of a pecan bar in her mouth.

"I'm happy you liked it. How about you, Summer? Want another Pecan bar?"

She answers with the loudest, longest burp I've ever heard coming from a woman. I start laughing.

"Sorry. It was pretty funny, though," I say to an unembarrassed Summer.

"Summer!" January scolds.

"I can't help it! I'm pregnant, you know."

"That was actually the greatest review I've ever had," I say.

"I hate to be a party pooper, but I'm going to stretch out in bed and watch some tv."

She gets up and pats her stomach. "The baby's moving like crazy. Goodnight, Sis."

January kisses her sister on the cheek. "Goodnight."

"Goodnight, Summer. It was great meeting you," I say and mean it.

"You too. I like you way better than Dick. Hope to see you again."

"Me too," I say.

She blows us a kiss and exits the room.

I turn to January. "See, your sister likes me."

"I like you, too, pal," she says, emphasizing the last word. Throwing the kitchen towel to the counter, she grabs the front of my shirt and pulls me to her. "Let's try this one more time."

I spin her around and pin her against the wall. "You're awfully bossy, my friend. I'm not your client, you know."

"You don't want to kiss me anymore?" she asks batting her lashes.

"Forget everything I just said."

I lean in and take the kiss. My tongue finds hers, and what I thought I knew about kissing evaporates into thin air. Her lips. They're soft and full, but more than anything, I feel like I'm the first man she's kissed this way. And in the moment the unbelievable happens. The sadness I've carried for eight years lightens. There aren't the right words to describe how I feel, only a reluctance to ever stop feeling this way.

"Maybe we can play an after-dinner game?" she asks, turning to walk away.

I catch her wrist. "I like this game."

She looks over her shoulder. "That one can lead to trouble. We need a distraction, we're getting off course."

The phone rings. She looks at the screen then at me. That fucker Dick's cockblocking me again. I know that's him. But in an interesting development, she doesn't answer and mutes the cell.

"Don't you want to get that?" I say, testing her intentions.

"No."

I'll take that one-word answer and the grin she's giving me.

"What about instead of games we just talk?" I suggest.

"Sure. I'd love to hear about your life," she says, grabbing the open wine bottle and two glasses.

We take a seat on the couch, and I motion to her to go first. My story never comes easy.

"Let's start with the basics," she says. "I lived here in this house till I went to college. Like I told you before, I settled in New York after that."

"What are your plans? The house, this great place, you're definitely selling?"

There's a funny look on her face like she doesn't know how to answer.

"I think so. New York is my home now. My biggest client's here, as you know. But I've got three east coast earners too."

"How'd you get into your field?"

"I was at a sports marketing firm. Worked my way up as their attorney. Along the way, I noticed where the real money was. And I knew I had a talent for what being an agent takes."

"Never married?"

"Oh, I was married. But it was a disaster."

"How so?"

"I ignored all those waving red flags. We weren't meant to be together. It lasted two years. What about you? Any youthful indiscretions you're paying alimony for?" She chuckles when she says it.

I take a deep breath and try to get my thoughts together.

January tilts her head. "That sounds bad!" She laughs. "I take it the answer is yes?"

"Usually, I say no when someone asks."

"Why lie?"

"I was married. Happily. For four years."

"Divorced?"

"No. She died."

I haven't said those words aloud for a long time. And the next ones for even longer. I have to spit it out; otherwise, they'll hide inside my heart for another decade.

"Her name was Katy. She had a brain aneurysm at thirty-two and died without any warning.

"Oh God, Brick. I'm so sorry."

"And she was pregnant with our daughter. Seven months along. The baby didn't survive."

As if on command, my eyes flood with tears. Instantly tears fill her eyes in response.

"It almost killed me. That's my story." My voice trails off.

She lifts a hand to her mouth. Tears stream down her face.

"It's okay. Come here," I say, bringing her close. "I cried for years. It took me a long time to accept that it had happened." I lift her chin and look into her shimmering eyes. "But thank you for that reaction. It's very compassionate."

I hold her. We sit silently, her head against my chest, absorbing what we now know. She, that I once loved another woman. Me, the stunning realization it could happen again.

CHAPTER 5

JANUARY

"Oh, Brick. It's lovely," I say, surveying the Swift property. This first glimpse wows.

His idea I meet everyone before we show up for the Halloween party was a good one. I'm curious. What kind of people raised a man like him? Every time we're together, I come away more impressed. Every time we're apart, I find myself thinking about him. His strength of character, the way he treats people. And I love how he can have deep, long conversations or just speak with his eyes. *Face it January, you're crazy about the guy.*

"This is where we grew up. Atticus rebuilt and expanded the house when he signed our first contract."

I'm snapped out of my thoughts.

"The trees! Just gorgeous," I say, scanning the Dogwood lined road leading to the home.

The house comes into view, pillars and porch reflecting the Southern Classic two-story design. Lime green and purple hydrangeas edge the home sitting atop a wide rolling lawn.

He parks his Mercedes on the brick circular driveway and turns off the engine.

"Before we go in, a few notes."

I almost start laughing at his businesslike tone.

"I love my family, but they're likely to be a little too eager to meet you. The Swifts aren't good at hiding their feelings."

I don't say a word, but force him by my silence to keep talking. It's one of my best negotiating tools. Silence always makes the other person say more than they planned. The funny thing is Brick knows this trick and most likely uses it regularly.

"Especially my grandfather. He means well, but he's gonna say something slightly embarrassing to you or me. Probably both. I apologize in advance."

I just smile.

"And he's not alone. Atticus and my sister Bristol don't have any problem saying what they're thinking."

"That sounds alright," I say, offering nothing.

"Your best bet is to talk with Charlotte or Mallory. They're still normal," he says as if he's perfectly serious.

"I'll remember that." My tone matching his.

"I mean, I had a talk with my mother and grandmother and asked them to not read anything into the fact I'm bringing a friend for Sunday supper."

He's nervous and starting to talk faster.

"It's just that I don't bring women here. I haven't, anyway. It's not that I don't date, but I never brought anyone here. Not that we're dating, but even friends. It's never happened."

Poor guy. I move the piece of hair that's fallen over his eye.

"Breathe," I say softly.

He shakes his head and grins. Then he blows out his tension with forceful push. "You're right. Nothing to worry about."

"I'm not a wilting, southern flower, you know, Brick. I can handle whatever comes at me. It's my thing."

"Good luck," he says, looking sincerely worried.

I wish I had a video of this.

He rings the bell.

Immediately a dog starts barking as if the castle walls are being breached.

"That's The Colonel, my grandparents' dog. He's harmless."

Footsteps approach the door. It swings open to reveal a tall, lanky older man with a shock of thick white hair and wild, untamed eyebrows. He wears a persimmon colored bow tie and a smile. An agitated dachshund is held tightly in his arms.

"Here they are!" he says, jiggling the dog who looks at me with a crazed look...

Brick places his is hand on my back. "January, this is my grandfather Davis, and that's the Colonel."

"So nice to meet you both!" I say.

Davis puts the dog down before he wiggles out of his grasp. The Colonel does circles around my feet, sniffing his hello.

"Colonel! Stop that!"

"Don't worry, I love dogs."

Grandpa leans in between us and whispers. "Before we join the rest of the family I want to warn January they may come on a little strong,"

That's funny, Brick said he was the one to watch out for.

"I'll keep them in line, dear. Don't you worry," he says, taking my hand.

"A girl can always count on a gentleman who wears a bow tie."

He looks at me with a twinkle in his eyes and kisses my hand. "You're a tall drink of water, aren't you?" Then looking at Brick, "Excellent choice, son! It's about time."

A soft groan leaves Brick's lips as we walk inside.

"Is that my Brick?" A female voice calls from the room up ahead.

"Yes, Mom. January and I are here."

Walking into the great room, I'm taken with the warmth of the scene. Smiling faces greet us from the kitchen to the conversation area. Brick wasn't kidding. He's made them very happy by bringing me.

"Hi. Everyone, this is my friend January."

All nine mouths sound their response. Hello, hi, welcome to our home, and more I can't distinguish . It makes me chuckle.

"Now that was an outstanding welcome," I say.

Brick goes around the room, making the individual introductions.

"This is my mother, Lucinda."

The striking woman with a dramatic grey streak walks over and takes my hand. "So happy you could join us, January."

"Glad to be here."

"And this is Boone, my husband, " she says, pointing to the good looking white-haired man joining us.

"Welcome. How about a taste of the heavens? I was just pouring myself a Jack Daniels."

For some reason, that gets a reaction from everyone here. There's laughter, and it's directed at the young pretty woman sitting next to an equally attractive teenage girl. The girl has a burn scar on one side of her face, but you can see she's confident in spite of the wound.

"Hi, January. I'm Charlotte, and this is my daughter, Mallory. That reaction is because of me," she says, rolling her eyes with some memory.

"Hi. Sounds like a good story."

The older woman smiling sweetly speaks up. "I'm Grandma Birdie. And that was all my son's fault. The first time we met Atticus' fiancé, Boone got her a little tipsy."

"She was drunk off her ass," says Atticus. "I had to carry her to the bathroom."

He gets an elbow to his side, and a playful half slap across his head from his grandmother who's standing behind him.

"She was!" Says the girl looking at her mother.

"That's Atticus sitting in the peanut gallery," Brick says.

"Great to meet you, January," he says.

"I'm Bristol," the beautiful brunette sitting across from them calls. There's such a strong family resemblance.

"Hello. Really nice to meet all of you. Bristol, I think you're my sister's obstetrician. Summer Calhoun."

"Oh, I love Summer! She's got such a funny sense of humor. All we do is laugh when she's in the office."

"She only has good things to say about you too."

"Dad, I'll take a drink," Brick says.

"I will as well," I say, knowing there's no chance of me getting tipsy.

This obviously pleases Boone. He pats me on the shoulder as if I just won a marathon.

"Good for you! I'll give you a little one to start."

His idea of little can use some work. But I nurse it for a good hour while talking with the family. They get to know me. Questions. Much to Brick's horror, there's lots of them. Where am I from? What do I do? Have I ever been married, kids? And when they ask if I'm living in Memphis permanently, they're disappointed with the answer.

Brick hasn't calmed down yet. I can see a new look on his face. He's uncomfortable with my being interrogated. Usually, his smile is easy and beautifully natural. But this afternoon he looks like he's waiting for the other shoe to drop. Like one of them is going to say something wildly inappropriate.

I don't think it'll happen. They're lovely and loving to each other. I'd guess all they want is for Brick to be happy. And for some reason that makes me happy too.

Lucinda rises from her chair. "January, can I steal you away for a few minutes? The girls are going to see if suppers ready. We're eating out back, and I want to show you that too."

"Sure."

Brick stands." I'll help."

"No!" Grandpa and Boone's voices say in unison.

40

Atticus laughs, and so does Mallory. Brick takes his seat as prompted.

With that, all the females get up and head for the kitchen. It was obviously planned. Brick sits back down and rubs his temple, and grandpa just smiles and nods as if the master plan's working.

"Can I pour you another?" Boone asks as I pass.

"No, thanks. I'm still nursing this one."

I follow the ladies into the kitchen.

"Whatever you're cooking, it smells wonderful," I say.

Grandma Birdie opens the top of the double oven, and the most glorious aroma fills the air.

"It's my Sunday Chicken, darlin'. It's ready."

"I'm going to show January our backyard," Lucinda says.

While the women move around the kitchen, getting different dishes ready to serve, Brick's mother and I walk to the double French doors. She opens them wide, and I get my first look at the Swift estate.

"Oh! This is incredible!"

We walk out to the massive tiled patio that sits on acres of rolling green hills. At the bottom are deep groves of trees that line the horizon.

"We've got seven acres of land. Two of them are our little forest.

On the patio under an overhang is a long table, able to seat twelve. It's set with Autumn themed china, and the napkins and tablecloth are various colors of the changing leaves.

"I'm speechless."

She chuckles and touches my arm. "I'm so happy you like it. I paint out here sometimes and never see the same view."

"Are those beautiful watercolors in the house yours?"

"Thank you. Yes. I've been painting since before I met Boone. Let's sit for a moment," she says.

We take our seats on the cushy chairs by the French doors. "I hope we haven't seemed too nosy today. We usually have better manners," she says.

"No! I've enjoyed your company immensely."

"You'll have to forgive us, January. We're such a tight-knit family, and we watch over each other like hawks. Brick has been the one who's life, well, it's been a long time since we've seen the light he had as a young person.

Her statement just about kills me.

"He told me you were good friends. It's nice to think something has made him smile again. I'm glad it's you."

I watch her face and recognize the look. It's hope. The one my mother wore for her daughters. Hope for our happiness. Hope for safety. Hope for love and a life as fulfilling as hers.

"I don't know what you know about his younger years," she says.

"I know about Katy and the baby."

She looks surprised and a bit happy. "He told you. That's good." She says it almost to herself.

Looking over my shoulder, she makes sure no one can hear. "It shattered him," she says softly.

Tears flood her eyes, and she tries to stop it by pressing her lips together. But one drop falls on her cheek and courses down till she wipes it away.

My heart breaks for her. And for him.

She takes my hands in hers and squeezes. "I know he's forty-one years old and doesn't need his mother to speak for him. In fact, he'd have a hissy fit if he knew that I was trying. But he's still my child. And I just want to tell you how grateful I am. Because whatever you are to him, friend, or more, it's enough for me to see him coming back to life."

CHAPTER 6

BRICK

*G*reen tights and a hat with a feather. Ugh. To make matters worse, a matching tunic so short and tights so thin it shows the outline of my dick every time I raise my arms. It's useless unless I'm standing perfectly still. If I don't come up with a fix, Atticus and Bristol are going to love busting my balls all night.

Agreeing to wear this says something about January's abilities of persuasion, and even more about my inability to resist her. It's getting harder to deny. I look ridiculous in this Robin Hood getup. But when she pointed out if I took the stick out of my ass, we might have some fun, I caved.

I park the car in front of her house and turn off the engine. Maid Marion's waiting on her porch looking good enough to eat. Whoever came up with that saying was a genius. Her fair complexion highlights the colors she wears. The loose blonde hair crowned with a wreath of pink flowers, the pale lavender dress draping from her long, lean frame. I'd like to wrap myself in the skirt. Better yet be under it, lips to lips.

She floats down the stairs and does a twirl as I'm getting out of the car.

"What kind of friend asks a man to wear this?" I say, palms open.

"A fun one, like me."

"You look great," I say, surveying the whole picture head to toe.

"So do you, my Robin," she says sweetly and in character.

"Oh yeah? What about this?"

My arms raise so she can see the flaw in our plan. She starts laughing.

"That's not the reaction I was going for."

"I don't mean to insult your obviously impressive jewels, Friar Fuck. It's just comically obscene." Her eyebrow lifts with the statement.

"What're we gonna do about it?"

She presses her lips together for a few beats before the words come tumbling out.

"You do realize you're always showing me your manhood, right?"

"I am not. Quit exaggerating."

"Am I? The pond, then here tonight. I think you want me to look. You're proud of it. Like a monkey," she giggles.

I just shake my head and control my smile. She may be right.

"Come on. Help me figure out how to hide it. I can't go like this."

"Can't you tuck it somewhere?"

She's serious.

"It's not that pliable, you know."

"This is the strangest conversation I've ever had," she grins.

But we're both holding back a laugh.

"Come on. We'll find something in the house."

Scene Break

I look down at the green print apron tied under the tunic, "Does this look right?"

She rings the doorbell. "Just pretend Robin's making dinner."

Shit.

The door swings open, and an eighty-five-year-old flapper greets us. Grandma Birdie is all fringe and feathers. There's a long cigarette holder in her mouth. Around her neck, pearls.

"Twenty three skiddo!"

"What does that mean anyway?" I say.

"I have no idea, darlin'. Grandma isn't that old, you know."

She takes January's hands, and they scope out each other's costumes.

"Birdie! Love the dancing fringe."

"Ohh, let me look at you! Absolutely stunning, my dear."

A song begins to play from inside the party. Grandma shakes her hips to the rhythm.

"What about me? Am I stunning too?" I ask, pretending to be hurt.

Grandma Birdie wraps her arms around me, as I knew she would.

"Well, honey, you're the most stunning of all. Now come in and show everyone how good you look in tights." She looks at January. "Don't you think?"

"I do."

"Why the apron, Brick?"

"It's a long story," I say.

"Really long," January says naughtily and under her breath.

I shoot her a look, and she shrugs her shoulders and chuckles as we walk inside. Grandma pretends she didn't hear. But I can see her holding back a smile.

The house has been transformed into a haunted mansion. Seating is pushed against the walls making each room a dancehall, and they're filled. It's always this party everyone wants to attend. This and the Firefly Ball. It grows bigger by the year.

January's taking in the decorations and crowded dance floor.

"Is that you?" She points to the large oil painting hanging on the wall to the right.

"My alter ego."

Replacing the watercolors usually hung on the thirteen-foot walls, are my mother's portraits of the Swift Family Vampires. We're a deadly pack of bloodsuckers who show our pale faces one day a year. All sharp-fanged with menacing expressions. We wear black high necked capes and white dress shirts, and each painting includes something portraying our individual personalities.

Grandma Birdie's wearing her pearls. Grandpa Davis a red bow tie to match the blood on his fangs. Bristol wears a stethoscope, and Atticus palms a baseball. Mother's self-portrait has her holding an artist's brush dipped in blood, and Dads shows him about to sip a Jack Daniels that's suspiciously red. Mine has me dripping blood out of the corner of my mouth while reading a contract.

The newest painting making its debut tonight shows Charlotte and Mallory as mother-daughter immortals. And even the animals are represented. Right in the center of the wall are The Colonel and Scarlett's portrait. This is the one to get the most laughs. The menacing vampire dachshund, lip curled up just as it is when he senses an intruder. But bright red blood drips from his canine fangs. Next to him is my father's cat, Scarlett. Evil kitty fat and lazy, with bloodied claws and a bored stare.

"This the cleverest thing I've ever seen!" January says as she inspects each portrait.

The room is crowded with dancing, drinking revelers. We weave through. I've taken her hand, so we don't get separated. That's the excuse anyway. In reality, I like the sensation of our fingers entwined.

At the opposite end of the room, I spot my parents dancing to *Spooky*. We'll say hello when the music stops. I don't want to wait any longer to hold her.

"Let's dance, Maid Marion."

Her eyes brighten. "Oh, yes! I was afraid you weren't a dancer."

"You don't know everything about me," I say, taking her in my arms and bringing her close.

We move smoothly within the space we have. My hand's on the small of her back, hers is around my neck. I smell the fresh flowers in her hair and feel the rise and fall of her breasts pressed against me. And I swear her heartbeat just quickened.

All of a sudden, these tights don't seem so bad. There's only a few thin layers of fabric between her body and my dick. I sold this costume short.

"Tell me something about yourself I don't know," she says, running her fingers across my neck.

I take a few moments before answering. "Here's one. I don't make friends easily."

A sly grin lightens her face. "You made friends with me easily enough."

"Is that really all we are?" I say, holding her stare.

She chews her bottom lip."I don't know anymore."

"I do."

Our bodies sway to a stop. All around us, people are dancing and talking. At first, I'm hyper-aware of what's going on. A woman is laughing loudly. A man close by just stepped on his partner's foot, and someone across the room is raising their glass in a toast. Then the noise quiets, and the people recede to the background. It's just January now.

"I don't want to be your friend, " I say quietly but surely.

"What *do* you want?"

"I want it all."

There's a pause before she responds.

"Our vow to not let sex ruin our friendship hasn't lasted a month."

"Maybe our new vow should be not to let friendship ruin our sex."

I press my body against hers, so she feels my intentions. Leaning in, I whisper in her ear.

"Goddamnit January. Don't make me wait any longer. Come home with me."

"I have no intention of refusing your lovely invitation."

A sigh escapes from deep within her as if she just exhaled for the first time since we met.

CHAPTER 7

JANUARY

*A*nticipation of a first time is a powerful pulling son of a bitch. It's making my panties wet. Once felt, you're a goner. I want him like an addict wants his fix... And the closer we get to Brick's house, the stronger the craving. It was inevitable we end up in bed. I see that now.

My pussy's on fire even though It's wet. I'm electrified with the fantasy of tonight, but the charge is thrilling. God. If this is my reaction to just the idea of sex with the man, the real thing might kill me. I've seen a hint of the length of him, a preview through swim trunks and tights. Lord and hallelujah, I'm in for a good buggering.

We've built this up to be something epic. Will it turn out to be all I've imagined? I'm pretty certain the answer is yes because it's not just my pussy telling me something wonderful's about to happen. It's my heart.

We've barely spoken since leaving the party. But he's holding my hand, and our eyes have said a volume. Every so often, he looks over at me, and when he does, I feel like a schoolgirl who just discovered the boy she secretly loves, loves her. Thrilling is too weak a word.

I think we're both afraid if we say anything this feeling might evaporate. So I take his hand and bring it to my lips, making sure he's real and not just a dream.

Lifting my hand to his lips, he returns the kiss. "We're almost there."

A final turn winds up a narrow two-lane road that climbs a hill. The higher we get, the better the city view; the more the twinkling lights bring the magic.

"This is a little bit of heaven, Brick."

I'm surprised when he pulls into a long driveway leading back behind a modest, older one story. It's a charming structure with a porch and a swing. The house sits on top of the hill, and the closest neighbors are on the street below.

He shuts off the engine and looks at me with stormy blue eyes. He's so fucking hot.

"I've never been as excited about being with a woman as I am right now."

His hand reaches under my hair and brings my face close. For a moment, he just looks at me. Then his mouth is on mine. Gently at first, taking soft, satisfying kisses. But it doesn't take long for the passion to build. His breathing becomes heavier. My panties wetter.

I feel his hand move around from my neck, down the front of my dress. My nipples harden with the nearness of his touch.

"Touch me, please."

He watches as his fingers graze over the gossamer fabric, then move to find my nipple. This sensation is everything.

"God, yes."

It's only a second or two before that hand slips down the front of my dress. I'm braless. His jaw tightens, and his hips lift just a little in his seat.

Leaning my head back, I take in the feeling. Hands pull my neckline down. I'm exposed.

"Oh god, " he says in a soft tone. "Beautiful."

Then his mouth's on my nipples, sucking and making them peak. Strong hands explore the shape and size of me. I can't help but touch myself between my legs, over the fabric. Rubbing. When he sees what I'm doing, he gets an exquisite look on his face, like he just had a sexy vision. Then I cross the line. I reach over and place my hand on his cock.

"Let's get inside," he says without room for refusal.

He covers my breasts, and we get out of the car as fast as possible. I'm practically running. He drops his phone and steps on it. I trip on my long skirt rounding the back of the house and almost take a header into a giant oak tree. Right there in the midst of our passion, we start laughing. Hard.

The view and the landscaping around the large pool are spectacular. I start to comment, but he covers my words with an indecent kiss. Our tongues, our lips, his hands on my face. It all takes away any opinion I have to offer. What house? Pool?

And all the while I'm pretty sure he's working to disarm a security system, without looking down once.

"Fuck!" He says, finally putting both hands and his attention on his key remote.

"What's wrong?"

"The fob sticks once in a while. Shit!"

I take the keys from his hand and toss them to the table next to the chaise lounge. That gets his attention. I'm making an executive decision. The time for waiting's over.

The wreath of flowers on my head goes first. I toss it into the pool, followed by Robin Hood's hat. They float away, linked together by the feather.

One piece of ebony hair falls over his forehead. I love that misbehaving lock. Everything slows down now. It's never going to be the first time again. I want to remember it all.

He unties the narrow braided belt I wear, and it drops to the ground. I encircle his waist, undo the apron strings and fling it aside.

51

Finding the hem of his tunic, I lift it just enough to be able to see the outline of his erect cock. He lifts the tunic right over his head and throws it behind him. Fuck me, sweet baby.

The man is a god in green tights. His manhood almost breaking through the fabric. We lock eyes, and he makes a grunting sound like a monkey. He has every right to be proud. Then he starts to peel them down, one inch at a time.

"Tease," I say.

"Want more?"

"Yes, please."

I come close and take matters in my own hands. I run fingertips across his bare skin from hipbone to hipbone. At first, I feel the length and width of him over the tights. I finger the tip and make him groan. I take his balls and very gently lift them in my palm.

Then my hand moves inside the tights. Before I even touch it, his cock is moving. Anticipation. It's taking us higher. My fingers wrap around his hardness.

"God. Yes," he says, pumping in my hand. "Kiss it, babe."

He peels the tights down and exposes his assets. I lean over and get up close and personal with the most magnificent cock I've ever seen. Jesus. I give him a peck on his pecker, just to tease. Then a lick all around the head.

"Wait! Let me take these tights off. They're cutting off my circulation."

"Not on your cock, they're not."

He grins and takes my hand, leading me to the patch of grass around the pool. Sitting down, he gets to removing the green laced shoes. I start to lower my dress from the shoulders, but he stops me.

"I want to do that, January. Just let me get this costume off."

"No hurry. I'm enjoying this immensely."

He's having a hard time with the multiple laces and the knots. So he breaks them off with his bare hands.

I straddle his legs and give him my best heated look.

"If you get those tights off in the next ten seconds, I'll give you a glimpse of things to come."

He lays back and peels the tights off in one quick movement. Now he's a naked god, resting on his elbows, ready to be rewarded.

"Well, clearly, I gave you too good of odds."

"Let me see," he says, ignoring my comment.

I make him wait for it. Just a bit.

Without breaking eye contact, my hand goes down to the skirt of my dress, and I start gathering it up very slowly. Brick's lost the grin, and his eyes have lowered to my hand.

When it gets close to the reveal, I stop. His eyes dart back to mine.

"Show me."

So I lift the dress above what can loosely be called my panties. They're so delicate and barely cover my lips. Besides that, they're mostly see-through. Not that I planned anything.

He sits upright the second he sees what I have for him. Awe transforms his face. I try to lower the skirt, but his head dives underneath. Then his mouth is on me, hands grasping my ass and pressing me closer. I could die in this moment and know without a doubt, I once knew the real meaning of pleasure.

CHAPTER 8

*P*eeling her panties down is my new favorite aerobic activity . I know my heart's pounding. I want to look. Fuck. She's my idea of perfection, everywhere. Bare except for the tiny patch of hair. Lips so soft and perfectly formed. When I separate them, her clit's visible and waiting for me. What a sight.

She's moaning as I touch every fold and crease. I press my lips to hers, and my tongue knows the way. She's incredibly wet. Goddamn. It tastes clean. It tastes like sex. No more waiting.

I kiss her one last time and come out from under her dress. Her face is flushed, and she's breathing heavily.

"You're beautiful," I whisper.

She sits right down on top of me and leans close.

"Fuck me right here," she murmurs.

I roll her over.

"How attached are you to this dress?"

"Not at all. Get rid of it."

I straddle her body, take the neckline in my two hands, and start tearing. The fabric's so delicate it hardly takes effort. First, the breasts are exposed. Her chest rising and falling with desire.

Pink aureolas and erect nipples all for me. I put them in my mouth, sucking one beauty then the other.

My dick's pressing against her, but a piece of the dress is preventing flesh against flesh. I lift my self up just long enough to gather the skirt. I rip it apart in a frenzy to get at her. Her pussy against my dick sends a charge through my balls, up my spine, directly to my brain. She spreads her legs, and every cell in my body cries out for her.

Without any more foreplay, she's as ready as I am. I balance myself on one arm and take my dick in the other. Running it up and down her lips, knocking on her door.

"Please. Put it in," she begs.

Legs wrap around my back, and I can feel her opening to me. I gently put the head in. Balancing myself with hands on either side of her. I'm holding back. Then I slowly push, carried by the slick of her juices. But it's fucking tight. Even with the help.

"Oh, god! God!"

"Too fast?" I say.

Her hands go to my face. We lock eyes. "No, I want it all."

I take her leg, put it over my shoulder, and adjust my angle. There. Better access. I push inside. She lifts up and down with my rhythm. She can move better than anything I've experienced. Fuck me, fuck me, fuck me.

Her eyes close. Starting slowly, I roll into her. Undulating with every thrust. She begins to moan. So do I. My dick's never been harder. I've never been as turned on. She closes her eyes for a few beats.

"Look at me," I say between breaths.

Her lids lift, and I'm staring into that blue lake. It's no longer serene, but wild and intemperate. The color of her eyes has changed with passion. They're darker now and burn with lust. It excites the fucking hell out of me. I'm part beast now, rising from her waters.

Is she getting close already? I think so. Thank God, because I'm not sure I have the power to hold back.

Her cheeks turn pink, and her nose crinkles with the coming of an orgasm. There's the sexiest groans coming from deep inside her. She pumps hard against my thrusts. My balls beat against her.. I hear my own guttural cry as we reach the pinnacle of pleasure.

Then it's all sensation. We come together in a rush of sexual fire frenzied by its desire to spread. My jaw tightens, her eyes squeeze shut.

"Fuuuuuck!" she screams.

"Yeah, come, baby!"

I pound into her with all the strength I have. There's no stopping me or her. Passion matching passion...

We take every last sensation the orgasm has to give. I don't slow down till that happens, resting my body on hers for a few moments before rolling off.

"I can't talk," she gasps.

"Me, either."

We wait until our hearts return to a halfway normal beat. I prop myself on an elbow and look at her. Just look.

"What exactly was that?" I say

"I can't say. But I hereby nominate you for the Fucking Hall of Fame. Or maybe the Kennedy Center Honors will induct you."

That makes me chuckle. I move a strand of golden hair from her eyes.

"That was the best. Best ever," I say. No contest.

She gazes in my eyes. "For me too. We're screwed."

"Completely. And just so you know, I can go a lot longer than that. No bragging just fact."

Her face brightens with the statement. "Give me whatever you've got."

"Now that I opened my big mouth, I need to tell you I need a few minutes. Maybe fifteen, twenty. I'm fucking forty-one, remember."

I think it's alright because her hand touches my face and fingers run through my hair. She's smiling.

"Wanna get in the pool?" An eyebrow lifts.

"Let me put some music on and get us some champagne. Sound good?"

"Meet you in the water."

With that, she stands and drops the torn pieces of her dress that still clung to her body. Arms in sleeves, the entire back, it slides to the ground. Walking towards the pool, she turns and looks over a shoulder. Am I watching? Oh yeah.

"Great beautiful fucking ass you have, Miss Jordan."

I get a grin before she dives in the still water. She comes up, swims back, and leans cross-armed on the pool's edge.

"Let me see yours. Give me a look," she purrs.

Shit. My dick just jumped. Getting up, I walk towards her till I'm standing naked right in front of where she floats. Her eyes lift and settle on my crotch . So I give her a dick wave. It's waking up already. Then I slowly turn so she sees the whole picture. There's a long cat call whistle.

"You're such a perfect little arrangement of atoms."

Making the complete rotation, I look down at my cock. "Not sure I'm gonna need the entire fifteen."

She giggles, and even that gets me hot.

"Stay there. I'll be right back," I say.

I head into the house, and the first thing I do is turn on the landscaping lights. Oh yeah. Now the pool's lit, the trees, and most importantly naked January. She knows I'm watching through the window and begins doing backstrokes. Mesmerizing. What a body. My hand automatically goes to my dick, and I take a long stroke. Memories of being inside her accompany the visual.

Better get to my job and stop touching myself, or I'm gonna come quickly again.

I start the backyard music and hear the first song on my playlist of favorites. Fuck, this is perfect. John Legend says everything I'm feeling. Not only have I not felt this good in years, I'm not sure I ever felt this way before.

Walking to the refrigerator, I take out the bottle I put in this afternoon. The flutes are waiting on the counter. I catch a glimpse of myself in the reflection in the sliding doors. Completely nude me, wearing an expression I haven't seen in years. Joy.

Gathering it all, I head back to her.

"Did you miss me?" she calls as I approach...

I set the glasses on the table and work to uncork the bottle like a naked sommelier.

"Like Harry missed his Sally."

"What are we going to do about that?"

"We'll figure it out. We're smarter and older, remember."

"It was only a movie. This story's real."

There's a second or two where we both realize how much truth is in the statement. The moment that lets me know we're on the same wavelength.

She grins at my expression and pushes off on her back. What a sight. Long legs, perfectly shaped breasts, and a pussy I'd give my right nut to fuck again. And the golden hair. It floats beside her like a blonde halo. But she's no saint. She's a misbehaving sensual woman and not afraid to show she enjoys it. I love that about her. I've never found feigning innocence appealing in a woman over twenty.

I carry our champagne to the edge of the pool and set the glasses down. As she swims towards me, I dive in. A shock of cold and then pleasure. I come up beside her and take her in a wet embrace. Naked against each other. Kissing. Umm.

"Lovely lips," I say, finding it hard to stop.

She breaks away and swims to the champagne. I'm right behind her. Literally. My dick against her, my arms over hers. We pick up the flutes

"Here's to the unpredictable wild world. And also, the shredding of the Jordan/Swift Friends Agreement."

She takes a sip and sets down the glass. Turning her body to face me, she rubs up against my dick with those velvety lips. I'm electrified.

"You're not playing fair. And I believe it's the Swift/Jordan Agreement."

"Let's not fight," she says, covering my face with soft kisses. "I've got a much better idea."

"Is it something I'm gonna like?"

She ducks under my arm, swims towards the stairs, and rises out from the water like Venus. Without looking back, she pulls her long hair to the side, twisting out the water. It's tucked up in a tight roll, away from her face. Even naked, she's surefooted. Sexy confident.

Turning to face me, she calls me with a finger.

"If you like blow jobs under the stars, you will. Come here, big boy. I'm feeling inspired."

Are there stars in the sky? I hadn't noticed. I only see her.

CHAPTER 9

JANUARY

*N*ovember and December have proved to be the hottest months of all. They melted forty into the new seventeen. This man. I may have to check into a rehab clinic for pussies with cock addiction issues. Although mine is Brick specific. I have no interest in other men.

Meanwhile, the time spent having sex over the last eight weeks must qualify us for some kind of award. Maybe Top Performers or Circle of Excellence. In the bed, against the walls, under the water in the shower. That one time on my stairs, which sounded sexy but hurt like hell. Him on top, me on top. Standing, sitting, floating, bent over, from behind, in the behind. *Ow! Oh. Ahhh.* We've been feasting on a smorgasbord of carnal pleasures like starving sex addicts.

But the delights of the flesh pale compared to what else I've found. When I crawled out from under the sheets, the truth was waiting. I'm in love with Brick. The moment I tried to tell myself I wasn't, was when I realized I was. There's no denying my feelings.

It's not just how he looks or even how he makes me feel. Not the sexy bedhead, the butterflies in my stomach, or the perfect physicality of him. It's the intangibles. Who he is down deep. He wears no mask with me. I see the man, his strengths and weaknesses, sure of himself but not in any way cocky. His character is rock solid. He listens.

Does he love me? I think so because the faint look of sadness I detected behind his eyes? It's not there anymore. And It feels like my fate. But that's a weighty word to throw around before ten in the morning. I have this nagging urge to tell him how I feel. To sing it to the heavens while skipping down the streets of Memphis.

I just can't bring myself to be the first to say the words. It doesn't help that it's only been two months. There's a possibility it hasn't been enough time for him. What if the thought never crossed his mind? That would be mortifying.

"I have to actually work sometimes," I say into the pillow. My words are muffled, but I don't want to move. The massage I'm getting from my handsome, naked masseuse is just too wonderful. He's straddling my torso, balls resting on my ass. Lovely.

He answers with a soft touch trailing down my spine. The chills follow his finger.

"Work? Why? We could live on…" he stops mid-sentence.

I look over my shoulder. The expression is priceless. He's surprised himself and doesn't know how to finish the thought any other way. What other word would fit? I'm not about to help him. He was right the first time. But if he can't even say the word, he doesn't yet feel it. I lay my head back down.

"I'm going to lock you out of my office today, Brick. I've calls to make, I need to go over a contract, and I'm meeting with Duane tonight to sign an endorsement. I'll see you tomorrow when you pick me up for the wedding."

"That's a little harsh. Who's gonna take care of my needs all night?"

We both break up with the question.

"Your needs have ruined my work ethic," I say.

He slides off my body and leans on an elbow.

61

"What about your effect on me? I haven't always been such a slacker."

I turn over and slip my arms around him.

"One more kiss before I go," I say. Before he can answer, I take the kiss myself and make it a good one.

"Alright. You win, Cruella, " he says, raising an eyebrow.

"Why the name?"

"Because you're abusing my dog."

I start laughing and don't stop till he kisses me quiet.

THE LAST DAY of December and it's a gorgeous one. Just a few more hours left of what will now be known as my favorite year. What a glorious way to close it out. As I dress, I'm thinking about Atticus and Charlotte's wedding plans. I fell in love with the idea. A private late-morning ceremony. Just family and I will be witness to the vows in the Swift forest. No best man or maid of honor. Atticus says the entire family deserves the titles equally. And being Charlotte doesn't have an extended family, these will be all the people needed. I think the whole thing's spectacularly romantic.

A home-cooked brunch will follow, and then the newlyweds will return to their condo and the rest of us to our respective homes until the night's festivities.

The reception will be at the Swift estate. All guests are instructed to arrive by eight and be waiting for the bride and groom to appear at nine. A New Year's Eve reception meant to blow out any other will be held under a huge white tent in the backyard. They even hired a live orchestra to provide the music. There's two hundred invitees, and Charlotte told me only a handful sent regrets.

I lift my reception dress over my head just to get a preview before tonight and attempt to shimmy into it. I'm trying anyway.

What the hell? This was much easier to do when I tried it on in the fitting room last month. It just slid over my body. Getting it past my hips, I look at my reflection in my mother's full-length mirror. What the fuck?

That airhead salesgirl was paying more attention to Brick than me. She must have wrapped up the wrong size. I flip the tag over. No, it's a six. That's right.

Shit! It hasn't been just sex Brick, and I've been feasting on. I've eaten more in the last two months than the previous six. The only positive thing about it is that my boobs have gotten a little bigger. You've got to be eating a whole hell of a lot to gain weight in your boobs. Ha!

Somewhere in the back of my mind, another possible reason begins to surface out of the fog. But it gets big and bold real fast. That's when I lose the smile.

When was my last period? WHEN WAS MY LAST PERIOD? ***WHEN WAS MY LAST PERIOD!!!?***

Instantly my head starts pounding. I'm cold and hot at the same time.

Grabbing my purse off the bed, I rummage for my phone. Before I access the calendar, I pause. And pray.

If you just give me this one thing, Lord, I promise not to ask for anything again. I just can't be a pregnant forty-year-old single woman. I'd make a terrible mother. Amen.

Just the words scare the shit out of me. It takes only a few swipes and taps of my finger to bring up the page I want. I move backward, starting at the end of November. No. So okay, it's been more than a month. Not to worry. I've gone five weeks between periods before.

My eyes dart to the previous weeks. Ohhhh shitttt! There it is seven weeks ago, big as day. What the hell, January? I didn't notice seven weeks had passed? Shit! Damn that man and his distracting cock, face, personality, self.

I'm screwed. Then I just begin screaming at the top of my

lungs. I throw myself on the bed and start crying. The funny kind where once every ten seconds or so you wail. Even in the midst of it, I can see the humor. It's like I'm outside of my body watching this crazy woman having a fit. My greater self is watching and telling me it's not gonna change things.

Then it slows to a whimper as I realize this doesn't necessarily mean I'm pregnant. Maybe I have some condition that causes you to skip periods. Yeah! That's probably it! Suddenly there's hope.

I need to buy a pregnancy test. Looking at my watch, I calculate the time remaining before Brick picks me up. Forty-eight minutes. If I leave now, I can be back in twenty. Five minutes for the test. That leaves me with twenty-three minutes for makeup, hair and finding another dress that doesn't make me look like a stuffed sausage. It's doable.

I grab a coat from the closet, throw it over my tight as a whore dress, and head out. Clear the roads! I'm a woman on a mission.

~

Back home, I unwrap and read the directions as I sit on the toilet. My hands are shaking. Okay, pee on the stick. Deceptively simple for something so monumental.

Urine runs over my fingers. Shit. *But God, if you grant me my request, I promise to be a better woman in every way possible. Amen.*

I wonder how many women have shot up prayers to the big guy while they were taking a pregnancy test? Suddenly acting as if you talk every day. Most of them I'd say, but for all different reasons and for two very different outcomes.

I'm just going to sit here and wait. My vow lasts fifteen seconds, then I can't take the waiting any longer. I leave the stick laying on a Kleenex on the sink and start pacing. Three minutes is an eternity when your entire future hangs in the balance.

Before the three minutes is up, I peripherally see the unmistakable lines. I feel the tears well up. My bottom lip is quivering like a child. But there's no mommy to comfort me or say everything will be alright. Nothing is going to be alright. Grabbing the cell from the counter, I tap the one name I know will help. The keeper of my secrets. I need my sister.

She answers on the first ring. "I thought you were at the wedding. What's up?"

"I'm pregnant."

She starts laughing. "Funny." Her laughter builds, as I picture her throwing her head back and touching her stomach. "That's great, Sister. Plenty of time for you to say goodbye to your perfect life."

When I don't join in on the joke, things get silent.

"January?"

"I'm serious. I'm fucking pregnant."

"Oh shit! Fuck! Is it Brick's?"

"Well yeah! Of course, it is." The last word fades away with my tears.

She goes into her protective mode.

"Ohhh, honey, I was just kidding. Of course, it's Bricks. And it's gonna be okay. Come on. I'll cry with you."

And she does just that. She starts crying right along with me. Soon it becomes funny. I laugh between sobs, she giggles between wails. Until we're both just laughing.

"Have you told the father yet?"

"Hell no! I just found out myself thirty seconds ago. Besides, I don't even know what I'm going to do about it yet."

She stays silent. When I begin to protest, she interrupts. "I'm just processing. Don't read anything into my silence. Shit. There's lots to consider, January."

"I haven't begun. Ohhhhhhhh"

"Want my opinion?"

"Yeah."

"Take a few days to think. Don't talk to Brick about it until you know how *you* feel. What direction you want to go. Then bring him in."

"Do you realize we have a wedding today, followed by the reception? It's not like we can skip it. Shit!"

"Listen. There's a big pink or blue elephant in the room now, and you're never going to be able to unsee it. You've got time to think things through. At least a little time. How far along are you?"

"I have no idea. I know nothing except for some unknown reason I got pregnant against all odds."

"Didn't you use birth control?"

"No!! I haven't for over a decade. I'm not able to conceive! Remember?"

"Well, clearly that's not true. It's sort of a miracle, January. Don't you think just a little?"

I start crying again.

"Let me just say one thing. Okay?"

"Yeah."

"I'm with you whichever way you decide to go. But I've got to tell you, being a mother is the most magical thing that can happen to you. Horribly, soul suckingly magical. The little shits. They ruin almost everything you have. Except love. That grows bigger than you'd believe."

Leave it to my sister to tell the truth, the whole truth, and nothing but the truth.

CHAPTER 10

BRICK

*S*wift weddings. Ours was in New Hampshire where Kate was from. That was fourteen lonely years ago. Lately, it's seemed like another lifetime. Odd. Because all this time it's felt fresh. Every day till January felt like the day after Kate and baby's deaths...

I never thought Atticus would be next up, or that so much time would pass before another Swift would marry. Life's random. I learned that young and the hard way. But that lesson has morphed into something new. Even though I know the randomness is still there, there's been a change in me. I'm beginning to think it's time to put the grief down. Let the memories soothe instead of wound.

AC blasting, I'm trying to cool off before getting to Januarys. She liked me in this white cashmere sweater and black pants. But it's fucking hot in the car. Even in December in Memphis.

Tonight might be the right time to tell her how I feel. I want it to be a quiet moment and not in bed. I want our eyes to meet and the words to spill out freely. She needs to know it goes beyond the physical. This happened quickly. God. It's definitely love, though.

Just her breath on my neck is proof. We have real intimacy. I'm too old to take that gift for granted.

Thinking of saying those three words aloud for the first time in years makes my stomach flip… In a good way. Excitement not fear. Fact is, I'm sure of myself. There's no reason to hide it now. There's still an hour before we have to be at Mom and Dad's. All kinds of time for my declaration and hopefully hers to change both our lives.

I make the turn onto her driveway, expecting to see her waiting on the porch. It's one of our things. But she's not there. Maybe she'll live up to what she said to me that first date. *Buckle up buttercup, I'm always late.* I chuckle with the memory. I began to love her a little that day.

Parking the car and getting out, I remove my coat and straighten the sweater. The front door opens.

"Hi," she says.

But it's with a different tone and an unfamiliar expression.

"What's wrong?"

She gives me a puzzled look. "What're you talking about? Nothing's wrong."

But she says it too quickly. And firmly.

I know that face. It makes my day begin. This is a new look I haven't seen before, like worry or fear. Something's off.

"You look beautiful. I love those white wool pants with the black turtleneck."

"Thanks. You look nice too," she says dismissively.

What the hell happened between yesterday and today?

She walks to the car and doesn't wait for me to open her door. She gets in.

Sliding in my side, I look to her.

"What?" she says, slightly annoyed.

"How about a proper hello? You don't want to give me a complex, do you?"

That gets me a smile.

"I'm fairly certain that's an impossibility. You're about the most confident man I've ever known."

I start the car and lean over for a kiss. "It's gonna be a great day."

It takes a few beats before she answers. "Yeah. Memorable."

It's mostly a silent drive to the house. And when she does talk it's about unimportant things, like weather and work. There's a sense she's trying to avoid questions.

When I pull up to the house, I miss my opportunity. Here comes Grandpa Davis to greet us.

"Look how cool he looks," she says.

He's in all black, shirt and pants, with a black and white small polka-dotted bow tie. We were told to wear white and black, so the pictures would look striking against the bride and groom and the winter forest colors.

Knowing the late December morning forecast, Atticus and Charlotte anticipated temperatures would be cold. They were right. It's in the forties. So we had instructions to dress appropriately. Actually, everyone liked the idea because tonight we'll be able to pull out all the stops for the reception.

January exits the car and walks into Grandpa 's embrace.

"Look at this pretty woman! You're gonna make the larks sing."

That's the first sincere smile I've seen on her today.

DEEP INSIDE THE SWIFT FOREST, we sit waiting. A circle of nine chairs surrounds the open space next to Charlotte and Atticus' plaque, where he proposed. Clever bastard. Now I'm going to have to think of something equally romantic when it's our turn. A wooden round is in the center. Leading from the round, back into the trees, is a deep purple velvet strip of carpet edged in a grey tone that matches the tree trunks. Lavender rose petals await the bride and groom.

Mallory sits in the seat next to Bristol and her latest boyfriend, Jeffrey. Grandpa Davis and Grandma Birdie are beside January and I. Reverend Michaels sits holding his Bible. Completing the circle is my father, who sits holding his Lucinda's hand. I take January's.

"You're so cold," I whisper.

Before she can respond, the music starts. So Close by Jon McLaughlin sets the mood.With the first notes, the Reverend rises and walks onto the circle. He stands facing the family. Atticus enters from the far side among the trees. His face reflecting what his heart feels. He looks great in the jet black cashmere suit.

Impatiently he waits, wearing his happiness on his face. And each of us here is smiling with him. Mom and Dad are already teary.

Beautiful Charlotte enters from the Dogwoods, pauses to look at Atticus, and walks down the rose petal-strewn aisle. My brother 's face lights when he sees her. A kind of wonder shows up in his eyes and by everyone's expressions, they see it too.

"She looks so happy," January whispers in my ear.

I quietly agree with a squeeze of her hand.

The bride wears an understated long white dress. But it's not made of typical bridal fabric. There's nothing gossamer about it. I think it's a kind of fine wool. I had a pair of pants I loved a few years ago that were made of the same thing.

Her sleeves are long and the neckline high, but it's very sexy because it shows what it's pretending to hide. My new sister in law has a good body. I can see by how he's looking at her that Atticus appreciates it more than any of us.

For the next fifteen minutes, we watch Atticus and Charlotte move closer to becoming husband and wife. Their vows are meaningful and touching, and there's such love on their faces.

Mallory's softly crying happy tears, Bristol has wiped away a few as well. Surprisingly my grandparents are the most in control. They just look pleased. But the person who's crying the most? It's January.

"You okay?" I whisper.

She can't even respond, but buries her face in the man's handkerchief she brought. I'm stumped. She planned on crying so much she needed an oversized square?

Reverend Jackson covers the enjoined hands of Charlotte and Atticus with his own. "I now pronounce you husband and wife."

Atticus doesn't wait for further instructions. He kisses his bride.

The Reverend laughs. "That's just what I was about to suggest!"

The family rises, claps, and calls out our love for the newlyweds.

January's still crying, but trying to make everyone believe it's sentimentality. I don't buy it. When I take her in my arms, there's no resistance.

"Come with me," I whisper.

Clasping her hand, I lead her away from the family who by now have surrounded the newlyweds. The trees hide us as we go beyond the well-worn path. I find a small clearing just big enough for the two of us to hide between the Dogwoods.

"Here," I say, turning my body to face her.

I take one long look into her eyes, and she dissolves into tears.

"Talk to me, babe," I say, taking ahold of her hands. "You're scaring me."

"What I'm about to say is going to change your life. And it has the power to end what we have," she says between sobs.

Involuntarily my skin puckers into a million goosebumps and my brows furrow.

The next words spill out of her quickly. "I want a promise that you won't have that horrified look on your face when I tell you. Because that would kill me, Brick. Just pretend if you have to."

What the hell is she going to say? How bad is it?

"Just please tell me you're not sick," I plead. "It's not that is it?" My stomach turns with the thought.

"No! It's not that, " she says, shaking her head.

"Then what?"

She locks eyes with me, and her crying softens. She lifts her chin with a defiant look. "I'm pregnant." There's a pause, and then, "And I've decided to have the baby."

Some moments in life are so stunning they quiet your voice and any chance of describing them clearly. My skin's tingling face to foot. And all the cells in my body are on high alert, attempting to absorb what just happened. At the same time, it feels like a space just opened inside me. I swear in this instance my heart grew larger, making room for the love of a child. My child.

Tears well without notice. Then the pure joy rises and breaks apart into a thousand pieces. I'm so goddamned happy. She melts into my arms and I pick her up and spin her around the small space between the trees.

"You're happy? Oh God, you're happy," she cries, hugging me tightly.

Together we cry like children do when you've surprised them with something so beyond their dreams they can hardly believe it's really happening. The sheer weight of the emotion is shocking.

I look into her eyes. "I love you, January."

She looks at me tenderly. "You do?" She says softly.

"You must know how much I do. You're the one."

"I'm actually the two," she chuckles.

A smile lifts the corners of my mouth. "Marry me. Let's close the deal." The words slide out so effortlessly.

Her lake blue eyes invite me to stay in their gaze forever. "I love you too. Yes, Brick, I'll marry you!"

She wraps the graceful fingers of one hand around my neck and leans into my ear. "Please always look at me this way. And let's vow every day to show our children what true love looks like. So when they find it for themselves, they'll never let it go."

No words of agreement are needed, only a kiss to seal our promise. And the whole misbehaving world slips away.

EPILOGUE

JANUARY

I suppose it was destiny that Brick and I would end up owning this house on this enchanted land. Its magic has entranced him too. Deciding to marry here was a no brainer. Today the pond is working its charm. I'm certain it's beguiling all who play in its water or even just look at its spectacular foliage.

It's been waiting a long time to come alive again.

There's a new family to welcome. And through me, one that connects to the property's past. I can't think of a better time to introduce them to each other than our wedding day. The happy faces tell the whole story. Adults, children, teenagers, beloved grandparents. And of course the furry friends of the Swift's.

The Colonel is sitting on Grandpa Davis's lap, on an inner tube in the shallows. He's looking satisfied because he's part of the action and high enough to see what's going on around him. Scarlett's asleep on the deck despite the music and laughter and general loud time we're all having around her.

Only Grandma Birdie and Boone are on dry land. One watching over the waitstaff as they begin to lay out the food, and the other attending to the barbecue and sipping on his beloved Jack.

The rest of the brood's exploring the ponds farthest reaches or balancing a libation and catching some sun as they float. Lucinda, Bristol, and Charlotte have tied their tubes together and are rowing in tandem around the entire showy perimeter. Mallory and her latest boyfriend look as if they're trying to sneak off unnoticed. But from here, I see Atticus watching.

More than once, singing has broken out as the playlist Brick and I made accompanies our day. It was my idea we include songs representing all the generations present. Top ten songs from everyone's high school years. Favorites from the fifties through this year.

Then Brick took it a step further and suggested we have every couple's love song as well. We decided they'd be playing while we share the wedding meal and hear the toasts. What could be more romantic?

It's been a hit with all the family. There's no better way to make sure people will enjoy themselves than to play songs they loved when they were young.

To that end, we've listened to everything today from Sinatra to The Platters, The Animals to Beyoncé. Grandpa and Grandma made us all laugh when they pretended to be loving the rap song Mallory included, by dancing in jerky, unnatural movements. Their idea of hip modern moves.

I decided to wait for an April wedding because of this place. Even though I knew I'd be six months pregnant and well beyond wearing a sexy body-hugging gown. But I love my baby bump and I'm proud to show it off. I may be a southern girl, but I've never been married to the rules of behavior set for its women. I know who I am. I make my own rules. Hence the fact we turned the day upside down putting the reception first.

Besides, it's always been my favorite month on the property. The trees are in full bloom. The white bell-shaped flowers of the Carolina Silverbell are so lovely for a wedding day. Flowering Dogwoods and Star Magnolias in white and pink encircle the pond. It's a riot of color and texture. The afternoon's holding a perfect seventy-seven degrees. By the time we say our vows at sunset, it should still be balmy.

The Swift's family roots grow deep, and tonight I'll officially entwine myself within them. In a few hours, I become January Swift. It feels so beautifully right. And the thought of our child growing up within the embrace of these people seems like a privilege. A gift.

Brick's wet fingers are entwined in mine as we float together among our reception guests. Me in my white bikini and he in white trunks. How very bridal of us. Leave it to Summer to find us a *Bride & Groom* float and matching hats for the occasion.

"Look at your sister," Brick says. "That's gonna be us soon."

Summer is standing at the entry to the pond holding a twin in each arm. She's still a ways from her pre-baby weight, but I know she's perfectly comfortable showing the little tummy that remains. All three are wearing sun hats. She's dancing to the music as her husband Guy swims between his other two girls and pulls their small rafts.

"I hope you're not suggesting we have four children! I'm forty fucking years old, remember."

"I'll be happy with this one," he says, touching my stomach and chuckling.

We're interrupted by the sound of the big bell. Boone's ringing it and calling for our attention.

"Dinner is served! Everyone out of the pond!" His booming voice goes well with the loud bell.

Grandma Birdie adds her thoughts. "Come on now, children! My food isn't meant to beaten cold! " she says waving us in.

Scene Break

The long rectangular wooden table set up under the white tent seats all of us. Everyone's put on their coverups or shirts and T-shirts. Brick and I are centered between Lucinda and Boone on his side and Summer and her family on mine. Grandpa Davis and Grandma Birdie sit directly across.

"Who wants more Wedding Cake?" Grandma says.

The moans of the diners rise.

"God, no," Atticus says leaning back in his chair.

"I'll have a little one," I say.

"I have no idea where you put it all, January. But God bless you, darlin'." Boone laughs.

"January, what made you and Brick decide to throw the reception first and then the wedding?" Charlotte asks.

"Heres the thing. We both wanted to have a pond party and the barbecue during the day, and a private ceremony at sunset."

Leaning forward, Brick makes sure everyone hears his thoughts. "I loved the idea of being able to have our privacy while still knowing you're all near. And you'll be waiting for our first dance."

"I think it's brilliant," Grandma Birdie says.

"Thank you both so much for making this day so unique and special," Lucinda adds, reaching across Brick and taking my hand.

"Look how beautiful you've made our deck and tent. Thank you, Lucinda.

Lucinda, the artist, asked if she could contribute to our wedding plan by decorating the dining deck and tent. What a beautiful job she's done. Flowers spill from the corners of the tent inside and out. She chose the shades of the flowering trees and then used what was opposite on the color wheel to compliment them. It's made our little family wedding look like an artist's canvas.

The first notes of Unchained Melody begin and Lucinda swoons. "This is our song!"

Boone rises and extends his hand to her. She's in his arms before the first lyrics are sung. They dance around the table, to everyone's delight.

"Will you still be mine?" Boone sings softly in her ear.

"See, this is where we all get our romance gene," Atticus says.

When they make one full circle around the table, they stop at their chairs.

"A toast!" Boone lifts his champagne glass. "Here's to the almost newlyweds, our Brick and his January. May they always see love in each other's eyes. That's all you really need."

"Here, here!" Grandma Birdie says.

We raise our glasses. Mine the only one with sparkling cider.

Atticus taps his knife against his flute, drawing our attention. "I'd like to add something."

Brick wraps an arm around my shoulders.

"Brother, you've not only made your bride happy today. You've made everyone here happy too."

Brick smiles his slightly embarrassed grin.

"It's like our family has one big heart. It's made of all of us," he continues.

I see Lucinda dab her eyes with her napkin.

"And for many years, our heart has been a little broken," he says looking at Brick with brotherly love. "Because you were alone. You can't say we all didn't try to get you to be a bit more social! Damn it, you're a hard man to push. "

The family's laughing at the truth of Atticus' words.

"But now I see you were just waiting for the right one. The perfect one. The only one for you. So here's to you, Brick. And thanks for being patient and knowing she'd be worth the wait. Cheers, brother!"

Now we're all teary. Grandma and Grandpa Swift are both blowing their noses. That is until their song begins.

"Oh, sweetheart! It's Twilight Time!"

She and her boyfriend of sixty-plus years are still moved by the music that first carried them away all those nights ago. It's touching watching them sing every word. Grandpa gives her a kiss on the cheek when it's finished.

"Now it's our turn to toast the happy couple," Grandpa Davis says. He stands and clasps the hand of his Birdie. "Our Brick was the first grandchild. We can remember the day you were born. You were like a little bird in our arms."

Brick is pressing his lips together, holding back his emotions. The entire family is on the verge of tears again and we're not even sure what Grandpa is going to say next.

"As you grew, we saw a fine boy, and then a man emerge. To say we're proud of you would be an understatement. Grandma and I love you deeply. And now, we welcome your bride into our family with open arms and heart. God bless you both."

He begins to sit and then stands back up. "Oh, and I don't think you'll beat our record of sixty-four years. Unless you plan on living to a hundred and six."

We all laugh at his challenge as he takes his seat.

"I don't think you're in any danger of losing your title, Grandpa," says Bristol as she stands for her toast.

"Hey, we have a chance!" Atticus calls.

"True. It's just Brick and me who are out of the running," she says. "But I'll bet the depth of your love for January will match any other love story here. And that's saying a whole lot. Everyone can see how much you adore her, and she you. It's inspiring. So I raise my glass to you both. May you always find your world in each other's arms."

Warmth radiates from every face, and it's all directed towards Brick and me. We kiss.

"Isn't it time?" he whispers in my ear.

I nod, and we rise.

"We're going to the house to get ready for the ceremony," Brick says. "Atticus, you're going to take care of Reverend Jackson when he arrives?"

"Go! I've got it."

We walk away from the table and onto the path. The family begins singing Going To The Chapel. By the time we reach the front door of the house and the song fades, my stomach is doing flips and cartwheels.

"This is where we part," I say. " Got everything you need? Remember to leave at ten to seven. I don't want to bump into you on the path. I want to dazzle you as I come through the trees."

"Don't worry, bride. I'll be waiting for you on the deck in an hour. We're getting married, you know."

He takes me in his embrace, and we kiss, saying it all with our lips.

* * *

ONE LAST LOOK at the clock in the hall and a check of my image in the mirror. Adjusting the circle of white baby roses that crown my head, I take in the entire picture. My hair falls long and loosely waved, the way he likes it best. The finespun fabric of the dress feels exquisite on my skin. It falls from off the shoulders to gather under my breasts. My torso encircled by a braided narrow rope made of the same material. Sleeves are full, but the fabric so light it hides its volume. The skirt drapes to the ground and covers my white leather ballet slippers.

As we planned, I send Brick a text. *I'm on my way.*

"Ready?" I say aloud as I rub my belly. "Let's go marry your daddy."

Grabbing the bouquet of pale pastel roses, I make my way out of the house and onto the path. Soon I hear soft humming. But it's not a record coming over the sound system. Brick wanted to pick the love song we'd use for our rowboat trip to the altar. The fact that it meant so much proved to me I'd picked the right man.

I'm pretty sure this one's being sung by the entire family.

Sunset through the trees casts a rosy glow as I approach where the path meets the deck. The charm of hundreds of twinkling lights hanging from the trees and placed on bushes melts my romantic heart. But it all pales when compared to my first look at Brick's face.

As I walk onto the deck, he's waiting for me. Handsome beyond dreams in a white dress shirt and sand-colored linen pants. When I notice he's barefoot, I kick off my slippers. His eyes lock on mine and send a silent message for me alone. *There you are, my love.*

"You look beautiful," he says, running his hand through my hair.

The humming turns to a song, and the whole family's singing it to us. Their arms are linked and they sway to the music. Over the speakers, I hear the original record come on, Here, There and Everywhere by the Beatles. I hear my own lyrics. Here. Making this day of the year. Changing our lives by the grasp of our hands. Nobody can deny that our love is here.

Brick comes to me and extends his hand. I wrap my fingers around his. Much of what we feel and say moving between us without words. He leads me towards the shore where our carriage awaits. As we pass the family, I see the emotion in everyone's eyes. And joyous tears. They're in mine and Brick's too. We're so overcome by the power and stunning romance of the moment.

Taking my arm, he helps me step into the rowboat that sits on the shore in the shallows. It's decorated with roses and satin ribbons that trail in the water. Two pale pastel velvet cushions pad the wooden seats.

When I sit, he pushes the boat away from the shore and jumps in just like we rehearsed.

The song continues, and the Swift singers know every word. Brick rows away from the shore and towards the sun deck around the big Magnolia at the far end of the pond. There Reverend Jackson is waiting to hear our sacred vows.

Brick looks at me and smiles, then sings his own version of the lyrics. "If you're beside me, I know I need never care. Because to love you means I need you everywhere."

I answer him with a promise to be his, today and tomorrow. I'll be here, there and everywhere.

THE END. To see the story of the only Swift sister, Bristol click The Cannon.

ALSO BY LESLIE PIKE

The Paradise Series
The Trouble With Eden
Wild In Paradise
The Road To Paradise

Love In Italy
The Adventure
The Art Of Love *

Swift Series
The Curve
The Closer
The Cannon
The Swift Series Collection

Santini Series
Destiny Laughs
Destiny Plays
Destiny Shines
Destiny Dawns

Lyon Family Series
The Beach In Winter
The River In Spring*
The Sky In Summer

Standalones (for now)

7 Miles High *

Royal Pain * (Cocky Hero Club)

Until Now (Happily Ever After World and Swift Family Crossover)

*Available in audio.

ABOUT THE AUTHOR

USA TODAY bestselling author, Leslie Pike, has loved expressing herself through the written word since she was a child. The first romance "book" she wrote was at ten years old. The scene, a California Beach. The hero, a blonde surfer. The ending, happily forever after.

Leslie's passion for film and screenwriting eventually led her to Texas for eight years, writing for a prime time CBS series. She's traveled the world as part of film crews, from Africa to Israel, New York to San Francisco. Now she finds her favorite creative adventures taking place in her home, in Southern California, writing Contemporary Romance.

Connect With Leslie:

www.lesliepike.com

Made in the USA
Columbia, SC
04 June 2021

38954259R00050